"It's amazing how I've become of the we working on this science project," Frank said. He took Molly's hand and gave it a squeeze. "I never thought weather could be so interesting." He smiled that flirtatious smile that made Molly's insides flutter. "Or maybe it's the company I'm keeping that makes it so interesting."

"Frank Sanders, you are a shameless flirt!" Molly announced, smiling, too.

Frank looked at her in surprise. "I suppose maybe I am." He shrugged humorously. "What can I say? I like girls! But I really meant what I said, Molly. I'm glad we're partners." And then he leaned over and kissed her.

His lips were warm and soft against Molly's, making her heart pound wildly. When they parted, he pushed her glasses up more firmly on her nose. "You'd better go inside before we get those glasses all steamed up," he teased.

After he had gone, Molly touched her lips in wonder. He had kissed her! Frank Sanders had kissed her, and Molly suddenly knew that she was falling in love.

Bantam Sweet Dreams Romances
Ask your bookseller for the books you have missed

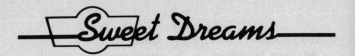

FAIR-WEATHER LOVE

Carla Bracale

BANTAM BOOKS

NEW YORK · TORONTO · LONDON · SYDNEY · AUCKLAND

RL 6, age 12 and up

FAIR-WEATHER LOVE
A Bantam Book / January 1992

ISBN 0-553-29449-0

Published simultaneously in the United States and Canada

Bantam Books are published by Bantam Books, a division of Bantam Doubleday Dell Publishing Group, Inc. Its trademark, consisting of the words "Bantam Books" and the portrayal of a rooster, is Registered in U.S. Patent and Trademark Office and in other countries. Marca Registrada. Bantam Books, 666 Fifth Avenue, New York, New York 10103.

PRINTED IN THE UNITED STATES OF AMERICA

OPM   0 9 8 7 6 5 4 3 2 1

To Darlene,
who's not afraid to be different

Chapter One

She saw him across the crowded marketplace. He was much taller than the men around him, and his dark hair had the sheen of a blackbird's wing. At that moment his eyes met hers, and Clarissa knew this was the man she had been waiting for all her life. . . .

"Hey, Molly!"

Molly Baker quickly closed her paperback and tucked it into a side pocket of her backpack. She grinned and waved at her best friend, Amy Stone, who was running down the front steps of Granville High.

"I was just about to give up on you and walk home alone," Molly said. She got up from the bench where she had been sitting and threaded her arms through the straps of her backpack.

"Mr. Raynor kept me after class," Amy told her. "He doesn't think I'm working up to my potential in math."

"You probably aren't," Molly said as the two of them began walking down the tree-lined sidewalk.

"You're probably right," Amy agreed good-naturedly, then groaned. "But I *hate* math. It's so boring!"

"It may be boring, but it's important," Molly reminded her, as she pulled up the collar of her down jacket.

"I think my problem in math class is that I sit next to Craig Wilson," Amy said.

Molly frowned at her friend. "What does that have to do with getting bad grades?"

Amy sighed. "Have you ever noticed Craig's eyes? They're the most gorgeous shade of blue. He's such a hunk that I keep focusing my attention on him instead of on those dopey math problems. I'd much rather work up to my potential in love." She shot a sideways glance at Molly. "But you wouldn't know about stuff like that. You don't have a romantic bone in your body."

Molly just smiled, thinking of the book she'd hidden in her backpack. Her romantic streak was something she kept well hidden from everyone, including Amy.

"So, anyway, Mr. Raynor said if I don't get my grade up, I might have to start working with a tutor," Amy continued. "He'll probably assign me to one of those nerdy kids who make the honor roll all the time." She flushed and grinned apologetically. "Not that you're nerdy," she hurriedly added. Molly had made the honor roll every quarter for the past two years, but she smiled to let Amy know it was okay.

Molly admired her best friend. Amy fit in with every crowd. She was sometimes thoughtless, often impulsive, but she was very popular, full of fun, and everyone liked her.

"Oh look, there's Craig now!" Amy clutched Molly's sleeve. "Wait here, I'm going to ask him something."

Molly watched as Amy approached the tall,

good-looking guy. Amy laughed and tossed her head as she spoke. Her long blond hair glistened in the bright sunshine.

Molly reached up and touched her own shoulder-length hair, wishing it were blond like Amy's instead of just plain brown. And it would be nice, too, if she didn't have to wear glasses, Molly thought. Molly was very nearsighted and had tried contacts a year ago, though the thought of putting little plastic discs right on her eyes had grossed her out. Even when she got over that part and actually got the lenses in, her eyes had teared so badly that she looked as if she were crying all the time. So she was stuck with glasses.

As Amy came back over to her, Molly noticed Craig giving her friend an apprecia-tive look. "What did you say to him?" she asked as she and Amy continued walking.

Amy giggled. "I pretended I didn't get the math assignment for tomorrow. He gave me the page number, then said if I have any trouble, to feel free to give him a call tonight." Her blue eyes sparkled with mischief. "You can bet I'm going to have plenty of trouble!"

Molly looked at her friend with disapproval.

"I can't believe you'd play dumb just to attract a guy's attention."

Laughing, Amy said, "I'd pretend to be totally crazy if I knew it would get Craig to ask me out."

Molly shook her head. "I could never pretend to be something I'm not just to get a guy," she said.

"You know, Molly, that's your trouble where boys are concerned," Amy said, exasperated. "You're too smart. You intimidate them. Guys don't care how brainy you are. They aren't impressed by the fact that you won first prize in the science fair last year and you'll probably win again this year."

"So what are you suggesting? That I *don't* try to win this year? You know how important it is to me. The Midwest School of Meteorology is offering a summer internship to the first-prize winner."

"I know, I know, and you want that internship more than anything in the world." Amy rolled her eyes. "Although why you would want to spend half your summer stuck at some boring weather school is beyond me." She paused, then continued. "It's just too bad you've got a reputation for being such a brain. I mean, *I* know you can be lots of fun, but most of the other kids don't. They think it's a little bit weird that you're hung up on all this weather stuff."

Molly shrugged. "Amy, I can't help what the other kids think, and I'm not going to pretend to be something different just to get a boyfriend."

"Oh well, it was just a thought," Amy said with a sigh. "So what are you doing tonight?" she asked as they stopped in front of Molly's house.

Molly pushed her glasses up higher on the bridge of her nose. "It's my night to cook, and I've also got a ton of homework."

"What are you cooking?" Amy asked. "Maybe I'll eat supper at your house. My mom is making tuna casserole again tonight. Yuck!"

Molly laughed. "I'm fixing meatloaf."

"Hmmm . . . your meatloaf or Mom's tuna casserole. What a choice! Maybe I'll start on that diet tonight."

Smiling, Molly said, "Well, you're welcome to eat over if you change your mind."

Amy waved and started down the street

toward her house. "Thanks, but I probably won't. I'll call you later."

Molly walked up the porch steps to her front door. She unlocked the door and went through the living room into the kitchen, where she dropped her backpack and jacket on the table. As usual, her mother had left a note for her on the refrigerator. It used to be that when Molly came home from school, she and her mother would sit in the kitchen and talk about their day. But that had been before Molly's father had had a heart attack. While he'd been so ill, the bills had piled up, so Molly's mother had taken a job as a receptionist in a dentist's office. She enjoyed it so much that she stayed on even after Mr. Baker had completely recovered and returned to work.

Molly took the note from under the cow-shaped magnet, smiling as she read it:

Honey,

Hope you had a good day. Chopped meat is in the fridge. *Don't* go out to your shed and forget it's your night to make dinner!

Love you,
Mom

Molly took the meat out of the refrigerator and began to assemble all the ingredients for her super-duper meatloaf.

When she had finished, she put the meatloaf in a pan, surrounded it with new potatoes, and covered the whole thing with foil. Then she put the pan into the oven, grabbed her backpack and jacket, and dashed out the back door. Almost immediately a small white dog ran over and jumped up and down, whining with excitement.

"Hey, Sugar. Did you miss me today?" Molly laughed and leaned down, allowing the little dog to lick her neck enthusiastically. "Okay, okay," she said, standing up. "Come on, let's go to the shed." The terrier mutt recognized the word "shed" and took off toward the small wooden building next to the garage.

Molly unlocked the padlock on the door of the shed and went inside. Sugar raced straight to his dog bed in one corner.

The first thing Molly did was set the alarm clock on the workbench. Too many times when she'd been out in the shed she had lost track of the time, burning dinner or forgetting a chore.

She sat down on the chair in front of the bench and breathed a sigh of satisfaction. This was her private place, where she worked to learn more about the field she'd chosen to enter when she graduated from high school. Her ambition was to become a meteorologist. She knew it was an unusual interest, but from the time she had been very young, the weather had always fascinated Molly. When most little girls had asked for Barbie dolls for Christmases and birthdays, Molly had wanted barometers and wind vanes, thermometers and rain gauges.

For a long time she had kept her weather equipment in her bedroom. While her dad had been in the hospital two years earlier, Molly had gotten the idea of using the shed as a weather station. It wasn't being used and in fact was on the verge of falling down.

When her dad was feeling better, he and Molly had spent several weekends replacing rotten boards and tarring the roof. They'd put up shelves and installed a workbench. Then Molly had added the personal touches that made the place her very own. Along with her weather equipment, the shed now contained posters, stuffed animals, two kitchen chairs that her mother didn't need, and a shelf full of paperback romances.

On the floor beneath the workbench was a small electric heater that Molly switched on. Within minutes it would take the chill out of the shed. She then set to work checking her various gauges and instruments and recording the readings in her log.

"Well, Sugar, the barometer is falling so we'll probably get rain tomorrow," she told the dog. "Let's hope the temperature stays above freezing so it doesn't turn into sleet." Sugar barked, as if he understood.

Molly laughed, but as she thought about her earlier conversation with Amy, her smile slowly faded. Molly knew that a lot of the kids at school thought she was sort of strange, and that some of the guys were intimidated by the fact that she was one of the best students at Granville High. But those kids didn't realize how important it was to her to keep her average up. Sure, there were times she would have liked to goof off, but she never lost sight of her ultimate goal of attending the Midwest School of Meteorology in nearby Indianapolis.

Molly had been thrilled when she'd heard

that the school was offering a six-week summer internship to the winner of this year's science fair. It would be a wonderful opportunity for her to get some real experience before she graduated from high school next year.

But Molly knew that she would have to get a full scholarship if she was ever going to attend MSM because most of her college fund had been used to pay her dad's hospital bills when he had been so ill. She also knew that if she won first prize in the science fair and was awarded the internship, and if she kept her high grade-point average, a full scholarship was a real possibility.

She sighed and adjusted her glasses, her thoughts returning to her best friend and their conversation that afternoon. Amy was always telling Molly she needed to learn to flirt if she wanted to get a boyfriend, and Molly knew that Amy had her best interests at heart. But she refused to indulge in the silly games Amy found so amusing.

Sure, Molly would like to have a boyfriend, somebody special to dream about when she went to sleep each night, somebody to think of every morning when she first woke up. She wanted a boyfriend who could make her quiver inside just by looking at her, a guy who was handsome and kind, caring and funny. And like Clarissa and Blake in the book she was secretly reading, when their gazes met, Molly would be certain he was the one she'd been waiting for all her life. But when she found that special guy, he would have to love her for who she was.

Molly reached into her backpack and took out *Love's Wild Ways*. *If I don't have romance in my own life, at least I can read about it,* Molly thought. Leaning back in her chair, she opened the book and began to read where she had left off.

The shrill ring of the alarm clock pulled Molly out of her fantasy world. She quickly shut off the alarm, then checked her wristwatch. Her parents would be getting home any minute. She closed her book, turned off the heater, then grabbed her coat and headed back to the house, followed by Sugar. As she entered the back door, she heard her parents coming in the front. "Molly?" her mother called. "Where are you?"

"In the kitchen," Molly called back.

"Ah, now that's what I like to hear," Mrs.

Baker said. "I hope supper's almost ready. I'm starving."

"I just have to put it on the table," Molly said as she set the table.

"I could eat a bear," Molly's dad exclaimed as he entered the kitchen.

"Sorry, Dad. You're out of luck. I'm serving meatloaf," Molly said with a grin.

"Darn! I really had my heart set on bear." He kissed her cheek and sat down at the table.

Molly went over to the oven and opened the door. The first thing she noticed was that the oven wasn't hot. It wasn't even lukewarm! She quickly looked at the knobs and groaned. "Uh—Mom," she said in a small voice. "I remembered to make the meatloaf, and I remembered to put it in the oven. I just for-got one little, tiny thing, though—I didn't turn the oven on."

Her mother smiled indulgently, while her father playfully patted Molly's head.

"Our absentminded Molly strikes again!"

Chapter Two

"As you all know, it's time to start thinking about the annual science fair," Mr. Welsh said, addressing Molly's first-period science class.

Molly had been making little doodles in the margin of her notebook paper, but she gave Mr. Welsh her complete attention at the mention of the fair.

"It will take place in exactly one month, and I'm sure you have all heard that the top student will be awarded an internship to the Midwest School of Meteorology," he continued, beginning to pace back and forth in front of the room. "Now, that gives you four whole weeks to put together your projects." He smiled wryly. "Though I know that last year there were several of you who waited until the last possible minute to throw something together."

There was a ripple of guilty laughter from some of the kids as Mr. Welsh went on. "I'm hoping to avoid a repetition of that last-minute hysteria by doing things a little differently. This year instead of working individually, each of you will have a partner." The classroom immediately filled with excited chatter.

"Quiet down," Mr. Welsh said, holding up his hands. Once the kids had stopped talking, he began again. "The Midwest School of Meteorology has agreed to extend the internship to both members of the top team, if both wish to attend. Now, I hate to dampen your enthusiasm, but you will not be picking your own partners. I've assigned them." There was a chorus of groans, and Molly's stomach jumped with nervous anticipation, wondering whom she would be assigned to work with. She turned slightly in her seat and looked around the room. Jessica Rendell wouldn't be too bad. Jessica was one of the better students and would work as hard as Molly. *Please don't let it be John Hughes,* Molly mentally begged, glancing at a boy who sat in the back of the room, his dark hair not quite covering his dark, glowering eyes. John spent most of every class either sleeping or grunting rude comments that usually got him sent to the principal's office. *Please, please don't let me get John as a partner,* Molly repeated silently, turning back around in her chair. She wanted a partner who would approach the project as seriously as she would, somebody who wanted to win as badly as she did. She crossed her fingers and focused her attention on Mr. Welsh as he began to read off pairs of names from a list. Molly listened intently for her own name, grateful when John Hughes was paired with someone else.

"Molly and Frank . . . Susan and Karen . . . ," Mr. Welsh droned on, but the moment he'd spoken her name and the name of her partner, Molly didn't hear anything else.

Frank Sanders? Molly thought angrily. *I have to work with Frank Sanders? The most important project in my life and I'm*

17

stuck with a jock who has more brains in his baseball bat than in his head! Without turning her head, Molly looked over at Frank out of the corner of her eye.

He was sitting sideways in his seat, whispering to Amanda Jenkins, the pretty redhead who sat at the desk next to him. Molly had to admit that Frank was definitely good-looking. His hair was dark brown, his eyes just a shade lighter, and he was tall, with broad shoulders and long legs.

As if he sensed her gaze on him, Frank suddenly met Molly's eyes. A smile lifted one corner of his mouth, and to her astonishment, he winked.

Molly closed her eyes in dismay. Frank Sanders might have been one of the most popular guys in the junior class, but he was also one of the worst science students. With Frank as her partner, Molly knew she didn't have a prayer of winning first prize.

"We have just a few minutes left of this class period," Mr. Welsh was saying. "I'll give you those few minutes to get together with your appointed partners."

The classroom erupted into activity as the kids paired off and desks were shoved together. Molly remained in her seat, waiting dismally for Frank to come over to her. After a minute or two she turned around and saw him laughing and joking with Amanda and one of her friends.

Fine, Molly thought irritably. *My partner is too busy fooling around to talk about anything as unimportant as a science project. What a total disaster!*

Scowling, she flipped open her notebook and began making notes on the idea she had been developing for her project. She intended to win that internship with or without Frank Sanders's help, and it seemed as if it would definitely be without.

"Hey, Molly."

She looked up to see Frank standing next to her. He grabbed a nearby chair and pulled it up beside hers. "Looks like we're going to be partners," he said, and grinned, the same self-assured smile she'd seen him give dozens of girls before.

"It looks that way," she replied coolly, pushing her glasses up on her nose.

"So, you have any idea what you want to do for the fair?" Frank asked, but it was obvious his attention wasn't on Molly.

He was smiling across the room at Amanda.

"As a matter of fact, I do," Molly said. "I thought we might do something with weather. I've got some weather-reading instruments at home, but I thought we could build other instruments ourselves. Then we could predict the weather for each day, using those instruments and keeping a chart listing how often we were right or wrong." Molly knew she was talking too much and too fast. She always did when she was nervous or angry, and at the moment she was a little of both. "Unless you have another, better idea?" she asked as an afterthought.

"No, yours sounds great," Frank answered cheerfully. "Why don't we go over the details tonight at the Dairy Barn?"

"The Dairy Barn?" she echoed.

"Yeah, you know—the place over on Fifth Street that serves all kinds of ice cream?" His voice was filled with humor.

"I know where it is," Molly answered curtly. The Dairy Barn was a favorite hangout for all the kids at Granville High, but Molly had only been there once with Amy. She'd felt very uncomfortable in the noisy ice-cream parlor, where all the popular kids sat at the tables in the back, laughing and carrying on. "Wouldn't we get more work done if we met in the library?" she suggested.

"No way! I can't work at all unless I have a banana split in front of me," Frank protested with a friendly grin. "Meet you at the Barn about seven?" he said as the bell rang. But he didn't wait for Molly's answer. With another grin and a casual wave, he grabbed his books and joined the crowd of kids rushing out the classroom door.

Molly gathered up her own books and slowly stood up. She had a feeling the next four weeks were going to be the longest ones in her life.

"I was starting to get really worried," Amy said at noon that day as she slid her lunch tray onto the table next to Molly's. "I thought I was looking at a Friday night without a date, but now I've got one with Craig!"

"Congratulations," Molly mumbled, unsurprised at Amy's news.

"When I called him last night for some math help, we got to talking, and he mentioned he'd been wanting to see the new horror flick that's playing downtown, and I naturally told him I was *dying* to see it." Amy began to disassemble her salad, picking out all the tomatoes and mushrooms and setting them on the side of her tray.

"But you hate horror films," Molly exclaimed.

Amy giggled. "*I* know that, and *you* know that, but *Craig* doesn't know that." By this time Amy had her salad completely destroyed.

"Why do you always buy a salad, then spend the whole lunch period picking it apart?" Molly asked irritably.

"My, my, aren't we cranky," Amy observed, raising her eyebrows.

"Sorry," Molly sighed. "I know I'm being a crab, but I can't help it. I'm not having a very good day."

"What's the problem?" Amy asked, drowning the remaining lettuce in her bowl with dressing.

Molly sighed again, more deeply this time. "Mr. Welsh assigned us partners for the science fair."

"Yeah, I know. He did the same thing in my class. I got Jayme Warren. We've decided we're going to make a working volcano," Amy said, grinning. "Her little brother has a fantastic chemistry set, and she says he'll show us how to make a big explosion." She nibbled at a lettuce leaf. "So did Mr. Welsh assign you some creep for a partner?"

"I got Frank Sanders," Molly told her glumly.

Amy's blue eyes widened. "Frank Sanders? You lucky dog, you! Craig is really cool, but Frank Sanders is the *king* of cool!"

"He's also about as interested in the science fair as he is in learning needlepoint," Molly replied.

"Who cares about the science project? You've got a whole month of working with Frank Sanders," Amy said enviously. "If you play your cards right, maybe he'll start dating you."

"Yeah, right," Molly scoffed. "Amy, you know Frank wouldn't be caught dead dating a nobody like me. He only goes out with cheerleaders and pom-pom girls." She hesitated, then continued, "I'm meeting him at seven tonight at the Dairy Barn."

Amy's eyebrows shot up even higher. "That's great! I happen to know he's not dating anyone in particular right now."

"That doesn't mean he's going to start dating *me*," Molly said. "He wouldn't look twice at me if we didn't have to work on this science thing together. I don't think brains are a part of the anatomy that interests Frank."

Amy grinned. "There's nothing wrong with the rest of your anatomy. You've got a good figure and you're really cute—when you aren't frowning and making your forehead all crinkly."

Molly touched her forehead. Sure enough, she could feel that it was all wrinkled. "I'm just not Frank's type, and he's not mine, either. I don't want him to date me—I just want us to do well in the science fair."

"Molly, you're hopeless, utterly hopeless."

Molly sighed. "Maybe, but I have a feeling that expecting any help from Frank on our science project is even *more* hopeless."

I should have insisted that we meet at the library, Molly thought as she stood just outside the Dairy Barn that evening. She'd driven to the place a few minutes before, but felt shy about going in by herself. At last she got up her nerve and walked inside, then paused, waiting for her eyes to adjust to the dim interior. The jukebox was blaring the latest rap song, and everybody seemed to be laughing and talking at the top of their lungs. How would she and Frank get any work done at all?

"Molly . . . hey, Molly Baker!"

She heard her name being called from somewhere in the back. Peering around, she saw Frank grinning and waving for her to join him and several other kids at a large table. Molly made her way toward them, clutching her notebook tightly.

"Hi. Pull up a chair," Frank said. "You want to order something? I can get the waitress over here," he added, starting to stand up.

"Uh . . . no, thanks," Molly replied. "I just finished supper."

"Anyway, Coach says we're definitely looking at a champion baseball season this year," Frank said, turning back to the two boys and the girl who were seated at the table. Although he hadn't made any introductions, Molly knew who they were. Ted Morgan and Andy Lopez were jocks like Frank, and the girl was Sandy Lathrop, one of the pom-pom girls.

"I can't wait till it's time to start practice," Ted said.

"Me either," Frank exclaimed, his eyes lit with enthusiasm. "I've been working on my grounding technique all winter long."

"We don't care how good you are at shortstop, just as long as you keep hitting home runs the way you did last season," Sandy put in.

As Frank and the others talked about the coming baseball season, Molly sat in silence. She told herself that after all, she couldn't expect Frank to drop everything the minute she arrived. As he talked, Molly found herself studying him. *He really is great-looking*, she thought grudgingly.

After a few more minutes of baseball talk, Frank turned and smiled at Molly. "I guess you want to talk about our science junk, right?"

"That's why I'm here," Molly pointed out stiffly.

"Okay. Why don't we move over there where we won't be disturbed?" He pointed to a small, empty booth in the corner. Molly nodded and together they moved from the table to the booth.

"I wrote out an outline detailing what I think we should do for the science fair,"

Molly explained, opening her notebook and handing him some papers.

Frank quickly scanned the pages, but looked up a moment later when somebody called his name. Amanda Jenkins and several of her friends were waving to him from across the room. "Uh . . . be right back," he said to Molly, jumping up and heading over to their table.

Scowling, Molly watched him as he talked to the girls. It was obvious he was flirting with all of them. She could tell by the way he smiled and moved. The girls were flirting with him, too, flipping their hair and fluttering their lashes. It all seemed so silly to Molly. She became more and more impatient as she waited for him to return to their booth.

When he did finally come back, it was only for a minute or two. Then he left again, this time going over to say something to a couple of other baseball players who had just come in.

Molly felt her temperature begin to climb as her annoyance increased. What kind of a deal was this? Molly thought that Frank had invited her here tonight to discuss their science project, but now it seemed that he was too busy socializing to have time for Molly or the project.

Well, I've got better things to do with my time than sit here and cool my heels, she decided, shutting her notebook and rising from her seat.

Frank hurried over to her as she was putting on her jacket. "Hey, where are you going?" he said.

"I'm going home," Molly replied icily.

"But we haven't gotten anything settled," Frank protested.

"I don't think we'll ever get anything settled here," Molly snapped. "I'm obviously intruding on your social hour."

Frank looked surprised at her sharp tone. Then he grinned sheepishly. "I guess I owe you an apology. Why don't you sit down and we'll start all over?" Molly hesitated. "I promise, you'll have my total, undivided attention," he added.

Molly relented and slid back into the booth. Once again she took out her outline and gave it to him.

This time when Frank read it, it was obvious he was paying more attention. "So basically what you have in mind is for us to build these weather instruments and use them to make weather predictions?"

Molly nodded. "I've got all the materials at my house. We need to start working on them right away. I was thinking maybe we could meet every day after school for about half an hour or so."

He shook his head. "Can't do it after school. I have a part-time job bagging groceries at the Save-Mart a few days a week. Most of my afternoons and evenings are pretty well shot."

Molly frowned. "But we have to work together on this."

"Did you know that in this light your eyes are the same color as a new leaf?" Frank said suddenly. His smile was so wide and so warm that it was as if the sun had come out from behind a cloud. Molly pushed her glasses up self-consciously, avoiding his gaze. Frank was flirting with her, the way he did with all the other girls, and she knew it didn't mean anything. But that didn't stop her from blushing.

"We're supposed to be talking about the project," she reminded him.

"Yeah, but your eyes are much more interesting," Frank teased. "Or we could always talk about how cute you look when you blush." When she didn't respond, he shrugged. "Okay, so when do you suggest we do this stuff?"

Molly frowned. "If you can't work in the afternoons or evenings, then I guess we'll have to meet in the mornings before school."

"When do you want to start?"

"How about tomorrow morning, say around seven o'clock?" Molly replied.

Frank looked appalled at the thought. "But tomorrow's Saturday. Why so early?"

"That's the time we'll have to meet to get some work done before school during the week, so we might as well start out that way," Molly told him.

"Okay," Frank said reluctantly. "I'll plan on being at your house tomorrow morning at seven."

"I guess that's it," Molly said, closing her notebook and standing up. "My address is thirty-two twenty-one Oak Crest Lane."

He nodded. "I know where that is."

"You can just come in around the back. You'll see a shed there, and that's where we'll work," Molly explained.

Frank stood up, too, and helped her put on her coat. "See you tomorrow."

Molly nodded and headed for the door of the Dairy Barn. Just before she left, she looked back and saw that Frank was sitting with another bunch of his friends.

It wasn't until Molly was back home, washing off her makeup before going to bed, that she thought of what Frank had said about her eyes. She took off her mascara and stared into the bathroom mirror. Without her glasses her reflection was a little bit fuzzy around the edges, but she could see the green of her eyes. *"Green as a new leaf,"* she said aloud. Funny—even though she knew Frank had probably said those very same words to every girl at Granville High who had green eyes, she couldn't help feeling warmer as she thought of him saying them to her. Then she gave herself a little shake. Frank Sanders was a dumb jock, a horrible science student, and a shameless flirt. So why had his words made her quiver inside with a curious kind of excitement?

Molly pushed those thoughts out of her mind and curled up in bed with her book.

*Clarissa knew Blake was an imperti-
nent scoundrel. He was also arrogant
and rude, and a womanizer as well.
She'd watched him at the governor's
ball, flitting from one woman to another,
bestowing his devilish smile on each
like a special gift meant for her alone.
Blake was not the man for her. What
Clarissa couldn't understand was why,
knowing all this, he still made her heart
pound so painfully in her chest. . . .*

Molly closed her eyes and sighed. She knew
exactly how Clarissa felt.

Chapter Three

Molly's alarm rang the next morning, and she quickly hit the button, hoping the sound hadn't awakened her parents. She fumbled in the dark for her glasses on the nightstand, then looked at the illuminated hands of her clock. It was six o'clock. She had an hour before Frank would arrive so they could begin work on their project.

Usually on Saturday mornings, Molly pulled on an old sweatshirt and faded jeans, not bothering with makeup or fixing her hair. But after her shower this morning, she blow-dried her hair and styled it, then put on just a touch of blusher and lip gloss. As she applied her mascara, she couldn't help thinking that her eyes were probably her best feature. Too bad all most people saw when they looked at her was her glasses.

When she was finished dressing, Molly saw that she had fifteen minutes to spare before Frank was due to show up. She quietly went downstairs and took her jacket out of the hall closet, then went to the kitchen. Sugar got out of his bed. Stretching and yawning, the little terrier approached her, his tail wagging so hard that his whole rear end wiggled.

Before Sugar could bark a greeting, Molly leaned down and scratched him behind his ears. "Let's go out to the shed," she whispered. When Molly opened the back door, Sugar scampered ahead of her and stopped in front of the shed, shivering in the frigid morning air. As soon as Molly let him in, he jumped into his bed in the corner and promptly went right back to sleep.

Molly turned on the electric heater, hoping it would warm the room quickly. Then she gathered together the materials she and Frank would need to build a wind vane. According to the instructions, it looked like the easiest of the instruments to make, so she figured it would be a good place to begin. Then she looked around, making sure everything was neatly organized.

The books! Molly thought. She realized she would have to do something with her romance novels. She definitely didn't want Frank seeing them. If he did, he probably wouldn't take her—or the project—seriously at all.

She looked around frantically and finally decided to put the books in an empty carton that she found under the workbench. As she was placing the books in the box, she wondered what the kids at school would say if they learned she was a secret reader of romances. They all would probably think it was hysterical.

It made Molly mad that her classmates had her pigeonholed as a nerd. Because she had a brain and wasn't afraid to use it, that meant she was boring, they probably thought. None of them except Amy ever stopped to wonder if there was more to her than good grades and hard work. It was just as Amy had said the other day—none of them had ever taken the time to get to know her and see beyond the label they'd pinned on her.

Molly finished packing up the books, then shoved the box under the workbench. She looked at the clock and saw that it was now exactly seven o'clock, so she went over to the one small window and looked out toward the house.

She hoped Frank would remember to walk around back to the shed. She didn't want him knocking on the front door or ringing the doorbell and waking her parents, who always slept late on weekends.

Tapping her fingernails against the window as the minutes ticked by, Molly waited impatiently. The sun was just beginning to show itself in the eastern sky, causing a faint glow of gold behind the lingering night clouds. Molly usually loved to look at the clouds. She had learned to distinguish the different types and to understand which formations predicted what kind of weather.

At seven-fifteen she took one of her books out of the carton and sat down. She'd read until he got here. There was no point just standing there at the window staring out.

By seven-thirty Molly was starting to get angry. She'd gotten up at six just so she could get everything ready for Frank, and then he was late. It just showed her how right she had been about him all along. He was rude and inconsiderate, as well as being a dumb jock. It disturbed her even more to realize how much she'd been looking forward to seeing him.

By eight o'clock Molly was livid. She had to face the fact that Frank wasn't coming at all. What a jerk she had been for taking special pains with her appearance. As if Frank Sanders would look twice at her!

She put the materials for the wind vane back into their box, then called to Sugar and stomped to the house. Taking off her sneakers but not bothering to take off her clothes, Molly crawled back into bed. Just wait until she got hold of Frank at school on Monday. Was she ever going to give him a piece of her mind!

"Molly . . . Molly, dear, wake up. There's somebody here to see you."

Molly opened her eyes and saw her mother standing in her bedroom door. "Huh?" she murmured groggily.

"Honey, there's a boy here to see you. He says his name is Frank."

Molly groaned and closed her eyes again. "Tell him to get lost!"

"He seems quite anxious to talk to you."

"I'll bet he is," Molly mumbled, reaching for her glasses and putting them on.

"Should I tell him you'll be coming down?" her mother persisted.

Molly nodded reluctantly and sat up in bed. As her mother closed the bedroom door, she got up and looked at her clock. Ten o'clock. Three hours late! How *dare* he show up now!

She ran over to her dresser and picked up her hairbrush. Her carefully styled hair now looked like a bird's nest. She suddenly slammed the brush down. Why bother to brush her hair or fix her makeup? She certainly wasn't trying to impress Mr. Three-Hours-Late Frank Sanders!

Molly stormed to the front door to find Frank standing on the porch.

"Frank, how nice of you to show up," she said sarcastically.

"Molly, I'm sorry about this morning. . . ." he began, an apologetic look on his handsome face. The morning sunlight danced on his hair, making the dark strands shine with hints of red.

"Don't bother making up some dumb excuse," Molly interrupted. "Frank, I know this science project isn't *nearly* as important to you as batting averages and stuff like that, but it's *very* important to me!" He opened his mouth to say something, but Molly didn't give him a chance. "I intend to do this project just the way we planned, and I'm going to win first prize at the science fair. You can either be a part of it, or you can ride along on my coattails!"

"Did you know that when you're mad you get two big red spots on your cheeks?" Frank said, a smile twitching the corners of his mouth.

Molly stamped her foot. "Frank Sanders, you aren't taking this seriously! First you were too busy with your friends to listen to what I was saying last night at the Dairy Barn. Now this morning you waltz over here three whole hours late, and then you stand there and make cracks!"

"I wasn't making a crack. You really do have red spots on your cheeks," Frank said cheerfully.

That did it. Molly lost whatever control she'd had. "Oh, you're *impossible!*" she yelled. Then she slammed the door in his face.

She leaned back against the door for a moment, trying to calm down. *I'm talking about the most important project of my life, and he's talking about red spots!* She raised her hands up to her face, feeling the heat that still burned there. Red spots . . . he made it sound as if she had *chicken pox!* Molly moved away from the door and sneaked a peek out the window. The front porch was empty. Apparently Frank had left.

"Molly? I heard the door slam. Is everything all right?" Mrs. Baker stepped out of the kitchen and looked at her in concern.

"Not really," Molly answered, heaving a deep sigh. "It's really not a problem, exactly. It's more of an aggravation. You know it's time for the science fair again. This year Mr. Welsh assigned us partners, and I got Frank Sanders."

"The young man at the door?" her mother asked. Molly nodded. "He's very good-looking. In fact, he looked like the type you girls would refer to as a real hunk."

Molly nodded. "That's part of what's wrong. Frank is cute and popular. Last year he was voted most valuable player on Granville's baseball team."

Her mother frowned. "I don't understand. What's wrong with being cute and popular?"

Molly moaned. "Everything. Frank's too busy being Mr. Popularity to bother with me and this science assignment. I went to the Dairy Barn last night to meet him so we could talk about our project, but he was too busy socializing to get any work done." Molly's face warmed as she remembered the strange way she had felt when Frank had turned his charms on her. "Anyway," she went on, refusing to dwell on that, "Frank is just a jock with no interest in doing well at the science fair. He was supposed to be over here at seven this morning, and you saw what time he finally showed up."

"Did he say why he was late?" Mrs. Baker asked.

"No, he didn't, and I didn't ask him. But I can guess," Molly said bitterly. "He probably stayed up till all hours last night, flirting with every girl in the Dairy Barn, or else he had a heavy date and couldn't drag himself out of bed this morning." She sighed in frustration. "Mom, you know how important this science project is to me. It's just my dumb luck to get stuck with a dumb jock!"

Her mother raised her eyebrows. "I've often heard you complain that the kids call you a nerd because you work so hard to keep your grades up. And now you're saying that because Frank plays baseball, he's nothing but a dumb jock." She smiled at Molly knowingly. "Aren't you doing the same thing to him that you hate having done to yourself?"

Molly considered this for a moment, then shook her head. "The difference is, I really *am* more than just a smart nerd, but Frank really *is* just a dumb jock!" she exclaimed.

Chapter Four

"Good evening, Blake." Clarissa hoped her voice didn't sound as trembly as she felt inside. She could hardly believe that he was standing right before her, his dark eyes gazing intently into her own.

"Hello, Clarissa." He took her hand and slowly brought it to his lips, then pressed a feather-light kiss there. Clarissa's breath caught in her throat. The back of her hand where his lips had touched burned as if she'd been branded. . . .

Molly sighed with pleasure. *Lucky Clarissa*, she thought to herself. She laid the book on the workbench in front of her, listening to the sound of the rain lightly pattering on the roof of the shed. The rain had been falling steadily for most of Sunday morning. Molly had come out to the shed to attack her homework, but the homework had been temporarily postponed so she could read one more chapter of *Love's Wild Ways*. But now that she had finished the chapter, it was time to start on her English literature paper.

She'd only been working for a few minutes when Sugar suddenly leapt out of his bed and raced to the door of the shed. His frantic barking told Molly that somebody was in the backyard.

She got up and looked outside, and her eyes widened in surprise as she saw Frank standing in the rain. In his hand was a bunch of bedraggled daisies. What on earth could he want?

She picked up Sugar, who had a tendency to nip at strangers who intruded on his territory. The little dog growled and wriggled in her arms as she opened the shed door a crack. "What are you doing here?" she demanded.

Frank swiped his wet hair off his forehead with the back of one hand and grinned. "I brought you a peace offering." As he held out the flowers, his smile changed to a frown. "Actually, they looked a lot better in the store. I guess the weather did them in." Then he smiled again, that appealing grin that lifted just the corners of his mouth. "Aren't you going to let me come in? It's sort of wet out here."

"If we'd worked together yesterday morning, I might have told you it was going to rain today," Molly muttered, opening the door wide enough to let him in.

"Hey, this is neat in here," Frank exclaimed as he stepped through the door, looking around the shed with interest. He looked down at Sugar struggling in Molly's arms. "Hey, fella," he said, reaching out to pet the dog's head. Molly was about to warn him that Sugar was not friendly to strangers, but to her surprise Sugar licked Frank's hand enthusiastically. *Traitorous little mutt,* Molly thought irritably.

"What's his name?" Frank asked.

"Sugar," Molly admitted, putting the dog back down on the floor. Sugar trotted over to his bed and sat, cocking his head to one side and watching them curiously.

"Cute name. He's cute, too," Frank laughed.

"Yeah, he is," Molly agreed. "So, what are you doing here?"

"I told you, I brought you a peace offering." This time he held the flowers out to her. "I'm sorry they got sort of wilted."

Molly took them, feeling a strange sensation in the pit of her stomach. No boy had ever brought her flowers before.

"Is this where you spend your free time?" Frank asked, shrugging out of his wet coat and draping it over the back of a chair.

Molly nodded as she carefully placed the bouquet of daisies in an empty coffee can. She hoped they wouldn't die before she could put them in water.

"And this is your weather equipment?" he asked, coming to stand in front of the area of the workbench that held her barometer and other devices. He looked at the chart on the wall, a color poster of various cloud types and formations. "Wow, you're really into all this weather stuff, aren't you?"

"I'm going to be a meteorologist. What's wrong with knowing what you want to do with your life and learning everything you can about it? What's wrong with preparing for your future?" Molly asked defensively.

"Nothing. Boy, are you prickly!"

Molly flushed, realizing she had come on a little strong. She pushed her glasses up on her nose. As usual, they'd slid down. "Ever since I was little, I've always been fascinated by the weather."

"You want to be a weatherman?" he asked curiously. "I mean, weatherperson?"

"A *meteorologist*," Molly repeated.

"Aren't they the same thing?" Frank asked, sitting down on one of the two chairs in the shed.

Molly sat down on the other chair and began to explain to him the difference between being the person who merely gave a weather report, and being the person who actually interpreted the data on which the report was based. As she talked, she noticed how the gold of the sweater he was wearing brought out gold flecks in his brown eyes. She self-consciously reached up and smoothed her hair. She wished she'd known Frank was going to come over so she could have brushed it and put on a little more makeup.

"What do you want to be when you finish school?" she asked when she'd ended her explanation.

Frank shrugged and leaned back in his chair. "I'm not really sure. I'd *like* to be a major-league baseball player." He grinned. "If I can't do that, maybe I'll do some coaching."

Molly nodded, unsurprised at his answer. She hadn't really expected to hear him say he planned to go to college.

"So show me exactly what we're going to do for this big project," Frank said.

Molly suddenly spied the novel she'd been reading before Frank arrived. It was lying out in plain sight on top of the workbench next to her English Lit book. The artwork on the cover left no doubt that the book was a romance. She'd die if he saw it. She would absolutely, positively curl up and die! Molly leapt to her feet. "Uh . . . before we do that, let me just put away my books and stuff."

She quickly grabbed her books and papers and jammed them into her backpack, hoping Frank hadn't noticed the paperback. When she had finished, she turned around to face him, uncomfortable when she saw the smile on his face. Had he seen it?

But all he said was, "You know, if you'd tighten those little screws in the frames of your glasses, they wouldn't slip down your nose like that."

She sighed in relief and pushed her glasses up. So that's what he was smiling about, not the book. "I know. I just never think about it."

Frank leaned forward in his chair, suddenly serious. "Molly, you didn't give me a chance to explain why I was late yesterday morning. The fact is, I overslept. I'm really sorry, but I just want you to know that I intend to work hard on this project." Then he grinned at her. "It shouldn't be too difficult, considering I get to work with somebody as cute as you."

Molly knew he was flirting, and she also knew he couldn't really mean it. But she felt a warmth spreading through her anyway. "I guess we'd better get started," she mumbled, knowing her face was as red as a beet.

As she showed Frank the plans and materials she had gathered together for making the various weather instruments, Molly noticed the pleasant scent of his cologne. When she demonstrated how to chart the rise and fall of a barometer, she noticed how broad his shoulders were beneath the sweater, and how long his legs were in his tight fitted jeans. In fact, for the first time in her life, Molly was having a terrible time concentrating on the weather.

"So the first thing we're going to do is make a wind vane," he said when she'd finished, looking at the plan she'd handed him. "Why can't we just use the instruments that you already have?"

"That would be too easy," Molly answered. "But we'll use them to check the accuracy of the instruments we make. After we complete the wind vane, we're going to make an anemometer."

He frowned. "A what?"

"It's a device to measure the speed of the wind. Then we're going to build a barometer and a psychrometer. . . ."

"Whoa!" Frank laughed. "It sounds to me like you're talking in a foreign language. Let's take it one step at a time, okay? Let's work today just on the wind vane."

"Okay," Molly agreed.

For the next hour they worked together, carefully constructing the wind vane. When they were finished, Molly assumed that Frank would leave. But he seemed to be in no hurry to go. He wandered around the shed and laughed when he picked up a stuffed giraffe Molly's dad had bought for her on a business trip when she was six years old.

"You know, this place is really cool, sort of like a secret clubhouse," he said, sitting back down in the chair and petting Sugar, who sat at his feet. "What else do you do out here besides work on weather stuff?"

Molly shrugged. "I come out here to do my homework, or when I just feel like having some privacy."

"Do you spend a lot of time alone?"

"Quite a bit," she answered. "My best friend, Amy Stone, and I spend time together. But she's involved in a lot of school activities. She's always joining some new club or working on some committee."

"Don't you belong to any clubs or committees?"

"I don't usually," Molly replied.

"Why not? A girl as pretty and as smart as you would have a lot to offer any club."

Molly felt herself blushing again. She didn't mind being called smart, not if she was called pretty at the same time. "I don't know. I guess I've just never taken the time," she said, busying herself rearranging the shelf of stuffed animals. She couldn't tell him that she'd always avoided extracurricular activities at school because she was afraid that the other kids would either make fun of her or shut her out.

Frank leaned back in his chair and put his feet up on the workbench, looking totally relaxed and at home. "I've got three little sisters. I'd love to have a place like this to come for some privacy."

"I always thought it would be neat to have brothers or sisters," Molly said, sitting in the chair next to him.

Just then she heard her mother calling, "Time for dinner, Molly."

Frank looked at his wristwatch and stood up. "Gee, I didn't know it was so late. I've got to meet Amanda in half an hour." He smiled apologetically and pulled on his coat. "She's going to help me with some of my algebra problems. I'll meet you here tomorrow morning about seven."

"Okay. See you." Molly watched as he walked out of the shed and down the yard, disappearing around the corner of her house. *So Frank was meeting Amanda and she was going to help him with his algebra. Yeah, right. And tomorrow I'm going to be voted Homecoming Queen!* Molly did believe that Frank was meeting Amanda, but she didn't believe for one minute that algebra was the only thing he'd have on his mind.

"I don't care," Molly told Sugar, who was whining at the door of the shed. "I don't care what Frank Sanders does or who he sees as long as he works hard on this science project. That's all that matters." But Molly couldn't help wondering why the image of Amanda and Frank together made her feel so depressed.

Chapter Five

"Hey, Molly, wait up!" Molly turned around to see Amy running down the school corridor toward her. "Gosh, here it is Thursday and I haven't seen you all week," Amy said, catching up to Molly.

"That's because you've been so busy," Molly pointed out as the two moved toward the cafeteria.

"I don't know how I ended up on *two* committees for the Winterland Dance." Amy sighed. "I'm in charge of ticket sales, and I'm also on the decorating committee. You should hear all the neat plans we have to decorate the gym." She cast Molly a sideways look. "If you play your cards right, maybe Frank will invite you to the dance."

Molly laughed at the very thought. "Not in this lifetime!" she exclaimed. "I'm sure he'll be asking somebody like Amanda Jenkins to go with him. I'm only his science partner."

"I wish *somebody* would ask you so you could get a chance to see the decorations," Amy said. "They're going to be awesome. We're even trying to rent a portable ice-skating rink for the night." As she rattled on about the decorations for the dance that was to take place in two weeks, Molly tuned her out and thought back over the past week.

True to his word, Frank had shown up every single morning. Even two days ago when three inches of snow had fallen the night before, it didn't stop Frank from showing up at her house bright and early. They had managed to finish the wind vane and the anemometer and were now working on the barometer. Usually, after they had worked for a while, they went into the house and had a cup of hot chocolate. Then Frank drove her to school.

It was really strange. Molly was spending

quite a bit of time with Frank, but she wasn't sure exactly how she felt about him. When he was with her, he made her feel all funny inside. When he smiled at her, her heart did somersaults. But when she saw him in the school hallways hanging out with his friends and flirting with the most popular girls, she reminded herself that he was just a dumb jock. They had absolutely nothing in common.

"Molly Baker, you aren't listening to a word I'm saying," Amy complained.

Molly smiled guiltily. "Sorry."

"I was just saying that you really should stay after school one of these days and work on the decorations committee. We always have so much fun." She picked up a lunch tray. "That way even if you don't go to the dance, at least you'll be able to see how the gym is going to look."

"I don't know. I'll think about it," Molly said, also picking up a tray.

"Oh, you always say you'll think about it, then you never do anything," Amy scoffed. "So how are things going on your science project?"

"Pretty well, I think," Molly said. "Frank and I are meeting with Mr. Welsh after school today to make sure he thinks we're doing everything right."

They paid for their lunches, then found two seats in the crowded lunchroom. The rest of their conversation involved their classes, and the latest gossip going around school.

After lunch Amy hurried off to French, and Molly headed for her geometry class.

"Hey, Green Eyes." She turned at the sound of the familiar voice, unable to prevent a smile from lighting up her face as she saw Frank coming toward her.

"Hi, Frank."

"Hi yourself," he said, with that special grin that made Molly feel so wonderful and warm. "I just wanted to tell you that I've got a meeting with the coach right after school."

Molly frowned. "I thought baseball practice didn't begin until next month." Was he trying to weasel out of discussing their science project with Mr. Welsh?

"Don't look at me like that," Frank said with a laugh. "It's not practice. The coach just wants to talk to me for a minute. I wanted to tell you that I might be a few minutes late for our meeting with Mr. Welsh, but I'll definitely be there. I wouldn't dare stand you up again—I've seen how angry you get!"

Molly blushed, remembering the morning he'd come to the shed so late and she had yelled at him.

Frank reached over and gently pushed her glasses up from the end of her nose. "See you after school, Green Eyes." With that, he turned and headed down the hall to his next class.

Molly had never been so confused in her entire life. She and Frank were as different as day and night. She was a brain, and he was a jock. He liked playing baseball, hanging out with his friends, and fooling around. She liked being by herself, reading romance novels, and getting good grades. They had nothing in common at all. Yet as Molly took her seat in geometry class, she couldn't help wishing that she was an airhead with nothing more important on her mind than what she'd wear for her next date.

"This looks really great, you guys," Mr. Welsh said a few hours later as he looked over the project outline Molly and Frank were displaying for him. "It looks like you're right on target."

Molly said, "By the time we finish making all the instruments, we'll have a week or two left to use them for actual weather prediction."

"Excellent idea," Mr. Welsh said, smiling at her. "Make sure you keep accurate records of all your data." Then he directed his attention to Frank. "And you're actually taking an active role in this project?" He sounded skeptical.

"Yes, sir," Frank replied.

"It's a fifty-fifty thing," Molly assured the teacher. "Frank's working really hard."

"Good. I want everyone pulling their weight," Mr. Welsh said. "Well, I guess that does it. It definitely looks like you're on the right track. And now if you'll excuse me, I have to run. I'm already late for my other meeting." He hurried out of the room.

"Thanks for sticking up for me," Frank said as Molly packed up the papers in her backpack.

She shrugged. "I just told the truth. This *is* a fifty-fifty project," she replied, then grinned. "If we don't count that first morning!"

"How are you getting home?" Frank asked as they left the room and headed for the main entrance of the school.

"I usually walk."

"You can't walk today, there's snow on the ground."

Molly laughed. "Frank, I don't melt when I touch snow!"

"I'll drive you home," he offered, taking her arm and directing her across the parking lot to his car.

"Really, you don't have to. It's not necessary," Molly protested.

"I know it's not necessary, but I want to," he insisted, opening the car door for her.

Molly got in and waited while Frank went around to the driver's side. She shivered, glad when he got into the car and started the engine, then turned on the heat. "It's gotten a lot colder today," she said, fastening her seat belt.

"I heard the TV weatherman saying last night that we're having an unusually cold February." Frank buckled his seat belt. "This heater shouldn't take long to warm up." He put the car in gear and eased out of the parking space. He was about to pull out onto the main road in front of the school when he snapped his fingers and looked at his watch. "I almost forgot—I've got to make a quick stop. Do you mind?"

Molly shook her head. "Where do you have to go?" she asked.

Frank was silent for a long moment. Then, glancing over at her, he said, "Valley View. That's a nursing home. I try to go there a couple of times a week and check on my grandma. It won't take long, but if I don't get there soon, they won't let me in. They're pretty rigid about visiting hours." He sounded almost embarrassed as he continued, "Uh . . . look, Molly, nobody else knows about this."

"I'm good at keeping secrets," Molly said softly. "But why don't you want people to know?"

He shrugged. "This is just sort of—personal, and I don't share my personal stuff with just anyone."

Molly felt a little thrill race through her. It was nice to know that Frank trusted her enough to share something with her that he hadn't shared with anyone else. It made Molly feel special.

A few minutes later he pulled up in front

of the Valley View Nursing Home. "Can I come in with you?" she asked impulsively.

Frank shut off the engine and hesitated for a moment, then nodded. "Okay."

They got out of the car and walked into the lobby. It was spacious and welcoming, like a large living room. There was a television set, a sofa, and several chairs. Some elderly people were watching the TV, while others in wheelchairs stared off into space.

"There she is," Frank whispered, pointing to a frail little woman sitting in a wheelchair in front of the picture window. "She likes to look outside. Come on." He walked across the room to the old woman and gently placed a hand on her shoulder. "Hi, Grandma," he said softly.

The old woman looked up at him with eyes that were the same color as his. Her face brightened and a smile creased her wrinkled face. "Johnny!" she said. "I knew you would come today. I told them you always come on the days when there's snow."

"How are you feeling, Grandma?" Frank asked, smiling at the old woman with a tenderness that made Molly's heart tighten in her chest.

"I had stew for lunch," the old woman answered, then she started to tell Frank about her day.

Molly stood aside while Frank and his grandmother talked. *Why does she keep calling him Johnny?* she wondered. As Molly listened to their conversation, she realized that the old woman's replies to Frank's questions didn't always make sense. She sometimes seemed confused and bewildered. At last Frank told his grandmother good-bye, kissed her forehead, and brushed a strand of gray hair out of her eyes.

Then he took Molly's hand and led her quickly out of the nursing home. He didn't say anything until they were back in the car, waiting for the heater to warm up. "It's hard to see her like that," he finally said. "She used to be real active and full of fun. . . ."

"Why did she keep calling you Johnny?" Molly asked.

"She gets mixed up. Johnny is my father's name. Grandma's got Alzheimer's."

"I've heard of it," Molly said, trying to remember what little she knew about the disease. "Doctors don't know much about it, do they?"

"It affects the brain and makes old people

real confused," Frank told her. "I try to come here twice a week to see her, but most of the time, like today, she doesn't know who I am. Half the time she doesn't even know what day it is, or where she is."

"Oh, Frank," Molly whispered. "I'm so sorry."

Frank was silent for a moment, and when he finally spoke, his voice was so low that Molly could hardly hear him. "When I was little, Grandma lived with us. Every winter she'd pull me on a sled in the snow, and whenever my dad was too busy to play catch with me, she'd come out in the yard and throw to me. She was so good to me—I guess by visiting her twice a week I'm kind of trying to pay her back for all the good memories she gave me." He laughed, but it was a forced laugh with no mirth in it.

Molly reached out and lightly touched his hand. "I think it's wonderful that you come to see her. It's so easy for kids our age to forget about old people."

Frank took her hand in his and squeezed it. "Thanks, Molly," he said simply. Then he released her hand and began driving toward her house.

As he drove, Molly looked at him thoughtfully. She'd thought she had Frank all figured out—a dumb jock who liked to flirt and play baseball. But now she knew there was much more to him than that. Her mother was right, she realized. She had been stereotyping him the same way she had been stereotyped by so many of the kids at school, and it made her feel ashamed of herself.

And Molly realized something else. The more she learned about Frank Sanders, the more she was learning to care about him.

Chapter Six

"Thanks for bringing me home," Molly said as Frank pulled the car up in her driveway.

"No problem," he replied.

Molly unbuckled her seat belt and turned to reach for her backpack in the backseat. As she picked it up, she realized she hadn't zipped it shut and her books and papers had spilled out. "Oh, rats!" she muttered.

"What happened?" Frank asked.

"Everything fell out of my bag."

"Need some help?" He started to unbuckle his seat belt.

"No, I think I've got everything," she

answered, embarrassed by her clumsiness. She zipped up the bag and opened the car door. "Well, thanks again for the ride. See you in the morning."

"A bunch of us are meeting at the Dairy Barn tonight for a little while," Frank said suddenly. "You know, just to hang out and have some ice cream. Why don't you come with me? I can pick you up about seven and have you home by nine."

Molly was surprised and puzzled. "Haven't we already talked about everything concerning the science-fair project?" she asked, as she got out of the car.

Frank grinned at her. "Molly, can't we spend some time together *without* talking about our project?"

"Well sure, but . . ."

"Great. I'll pick you up about seven." With that, he waved and drove off.

Molly slowly turned and walked toward her house, her thoughts whirling dizzily.

He'd asked her to go with him to the Dairy Barn, and it had nothing to do with the science project. He'd made it sound as if he just wanted to be with her. He'd made it sound almost like a date. Molly unlocked the front door and stepped inside, still stunned. She actually had a date with Frank Sanders!

At quarter of seven that evening, Molly stood in front of the mirror in her bedroom, staring critically at her reflection. She'd changed her clothes three times before she'd finally settled on the outfit she was wearing. She smiled, satisfied that she'd made a good choice. The pale green sweater brought out the green in her eyes and made her hair look darker and richer. Her new stone-washed jeans hugged her legs with just the right amount of tightness. Excitement added color to her cheeks and sparkle to her eyes behind her glasses.

Molly just couldn't believe that Frank had really invited her to go out with him this evening. All of his friends would be there. What would they think when they saw Brainy Molly Baker out with Frank Sanders? It was suddenly very important to Molly that Frank's friends like her.

She jumped as a knock sounded on her door.

"Honey, Frank's here," her mother said, popping her head into the room. "Oh, Molly dear, you look so nice!" She smiled her approval. "Now, you'll be home around nine, right? After all, it *is* a school night."

Molly nodded. "I know. Are you *sure* I look all right?"

"You look lovely," Mrs. Baker assured her, kissing her on the forehead. "Have a wonderful time."

With one last look in the mirror, Molly left her bedroom and went into the living room, where she found Frank talking to her father.

"What position do you play?" Mr. Baker was asking Frank as she came in.

"Shortstop," Frank told him. "I think we'll have a really good team this year. . . ."

"Hi," Molly said shyly, interrupting the conversation before they got totally engrossed in baseball talk.

"Oh, hi." Frank stood up and smiled. "You all ready?"

She nodded and Frank turned back to her father. "It was nice meeting you, Mr. Baker. I'll have Molly home by nine."

"Have fun," Mrs. Baker called after them as Molly grabbed her coat and left the house with Frank.

"I like your parents," Frank said as they walked to his car.

Molly smiled. "Yeah, they're pretty terrific. My dad had a heart attack two years ago, and it was pretty scary. It made me appreciate him a whole lot more."

Frank leaned against the car door, his expression serious. "I guess you never really appreciate what you've got until it's gone. That's sort of the way I feel about my grandma. I wish I'd spent more time with her before she got so sick." He opened the car door. "We'd better get over to the Dairy Barn before it's time to bring you back home."

It took only a few minutes to drive to the ice-cream parlor. On the way they talked about school and the people they both knew. Molly hoped she didn't sound as nervous as she felt. Her stomach felt as if it were filled with a dozen butterflies as they pulled into the parking lot of the Dairy Barn.

When they got out of the car, Frank took Molly's hand in his, as if it were the most natural thing in the world. His hand was warm, his grasp firm, and it made Molly feel less nervous.

As soon as they entered the ice-cream

place, Frank immediately spotted a table of his friends in the back. "Come on," he said, pulling Molly along with him. "Hi, guys," he greeted the kids at the table. "You all know Molly Baker, right?" he added, pulling up two more chairs.

Molly murmured "Hello" as she and Frank sat down. She recognized all the kids. Sandy Lathrop was there with Jerry Minter, one of Frank's baseball buddies. Now Sandy smiled at Molly. "Aren't you in my American history class?" she asked.

Molly nodded. "Yes, I sit two rows behind you."

"Mr. Williams put me in the front row because he says I have a talking problem." Sandy laughed and made a face. "I don't have a talking problem—I talk just fine!"

"That's the problem," Jerry replied, making an expression of mock pain as Sandy jabbed him in the ribs.

"What do you want to eat, Molly?" Frank asked as the waitress came over to their table.

Molly shrugged. "I don't know. What are you getting?"

"A super-duper banana split," Frank replied. "Want one?"

Molly shook her head. "I could never eat all that! How about a small hot-fudge sundae?"

"Okay." Frank gave their order to the waitress.

"You hang out with Amy Stone, don't you?" Sandy asked when the waitress had gone.

"She's my best friend," Molly answered.

"I'm working with her on the decorations committee for the Winterland Dance," Sandy said. "Amy's a lot of fun."

"Yeah, Amy can be a character." Molly paused, then continued, "I hear the decorations are really going to be super."

"Are you going to the dance?" Sandy asked Frank.

Frank shrugged. "I haven't decided yet."

His answer made Molly's ears perk up. Did that mean he hadn't asked anybody to the dance yet? *Take it easy,* she told herself. *Just because Frank asked you out for ice cream doesn't mean he's going to invite you to the Winterland Dance.* Still, she couldn't help the little shiver of pleasure that ran through her at the thought of dancing with Frank across the gym floor. It was a wonderful fantasy, but that's all it was . . . a fantasy.

At that moment the waitress arrived with

Frank's banana split and Molly's sundae. While Molly ate, she listened to the other kids talking and joking with each other.

"Didn't you win first prize in the science fair last year?" Stan Washburn, another member of the baseball team, asked Molly.

"Yes," she answered, feeling a tight knot of apprehension in the pit of her stomach. Were they going to tease her? Make fun of her for being a brain?

"You made a hurricane in a glass case, didn't you?" Bob Myers asked.

Molly nodded silently. If they started to laugh at her, she didn't know what she'd do.

"I thought that was really cool," Stan said. "How did you ever think of doing something like that?"

"Molly's really into the weather . . . it's her main hobby," Frank interjected, smiling at her warmly. "You should see the awesome workshop she has in her backyard, with all kinds of equipment."

"What other hobbies do you have?" Sandy asked curiously.

Molly wished she could say something really exciting, like that she was into hang gliding or motorcycle racing. But the truth was, she didn't really have any other hobbies except reading romance novels, and she certainly wasn't going to admit that.

"Molly likes to do lots of things," Frank answered, coming to her rescue. "She especially likes to eat hot-fudge sundaes. But if she doesn't hurry up, I'm going to eat the rest of my banana split and her sundae as well!"

With a laugh Molly put a spoonful of the sundae into her mouth, grateful when everyone began talking about the different kinds of ice cream they liked. From there the talk turned to favorite and least-favorite subjects and teachers. Molly was surprised to find herself joining in the conversation. She was actually having fun! *These kids are really nice*, she marveled.

She was disappointed when Frank touched her on the arm and gestured to his wristwatch. "I'd better get you home. I don't want to make your parents mad at me the first time I take you out."

Although Molly was sorry that it was time to leave, Frank's words thrilled her because they implied that there might be other times when he would ask her out.

"Hey, Molly, why don't you stay after school one of these days and help us with the decorating committee?" Sandy said as Molly and Frank stood up to leave. "We can always use another pair of hands."

"I just might do that," Molly replied with a smile.

"I like your friends," she told Frank when they were in his car on the way back to her house.

"Yeah, they're a good bunch," he agreed. "Hey, look at that! It's snowing, just the way we predicted it would!" He sounded delighted.

Molly laughed. "I guess you like snow, huh?"

"I like winter," Frank said, then added, "but it's amazing how much more conscious I've become of the weather since we started working on this project."

He took her hand and gave it a squeeze. "I never thought weather could be so interesting." He smiled that flirtatious smile that made Molly's insides flutter. "Or maybe it's the company I'm keeping that makes it so interesting."

"Frank Sanders, you are a shameless flirt!" Molly announced, smiling too.

Frank looked at her in surprise, then pulled into her driveway and turned off the engine. "I suppose maybe I am." He shrugged humorously. "What can I say? I like girls! But I really meant what I said, Molly. I'm glad we're partners." And then he leaned over and kissed her.

His lips were warm and soft against Molly's, making her heart pound wildly. When they parted, he pushed her glasses up more firmly on her nose. "You'd better go inside before we get those glasses all steamed up," he teased.

Numbed by his kiss and dazed by all the crazy emotions whirling around inside her, Molly murmured, "Uh . . . thanks for the ice cream," and got out of the car.

"See you in the morning, Green Eyes," Frank called out the window as he drove off.

Molly stood on the front porch for a long moment after he had gone. She touched her lips in wonder, convinced that she could still feel the warmth of his kiss. "Green Eyes" . . . she loved the way he said it, as if it were a special nickname just for her. She'd never felt like this before, all hot and cold, shivery and feverish. She felt as if she could dance on air, climb a mountain, float on a cloud. He had kissed her! Frank Sanders had kissed her, and Molly suddenly knew that she was falling in love.

Chapter Seven

"Hey Molly, hand me some more of those snowflakes," Amy called down from atop the ladder where she was perched. She was hanging plastic snowflakes from strings suspended from the ceiling of the girls' gym.

"Okay." Molly went over to a table where, among the crepe paper and posters, paints and glitter, she found a pile of big snowflakes. Grabbing a handful, she hurried back over to Amy and handed them to her.

"Thanks," Amy said. She grinned at Molly. "I'm glad you actually decided to help with the decorations."

79

"So am I," Molly said with an answering grin.

After her date with Frank last night, she'd felt so happy that she'd decided to stay after school today and help the decorating committee. Everybody had seemed really glad to see her, and Sandy Lathrop had been especially nice.

Molly had lain awake half the night, reliving the magic of Frank's kiss in her mind. When he had come to her house that morning to work on their project, Molly had felt sort of shy. She wasn't sure how she was supposed to act with the guy who had kissed her so wonderfully the night before. But Frank had immediately put her at ease, joking, teasing, and smiling at her with that special smile.

Sandy called from across the gym, and Molly hurried over to where Sandy was painting a snow scene on a big flat. "Want to help me paint this scene?" Sandy asked with a friendly smile. "Greg Jeffries drew the fence post and trees, but I could use a hand filling it in."

"Why don't you just paint it all white and title it 'Blizzard'?" Molly joked.

"Oh, a real comedian," Sandy laughed, threatening Molly with her paintbrush.

Molly picked up another brush and stared at the scene thoughtfully. Noticing the clouds Greg had penciled in, she murmured, "The clouds are all wrong."

"Huh?" Sandy looked at her curiously.

"The clouds—they're all wrong. Greg drew cumulus clouds." She grinned at Sandy's look of confusion. "Cumulus clouds bring thunderstorms, not snow. Since this is a winter scene, there should be stratus clouds."

"Wow, it's terrific that you know that stuff," Sandy said in admiration. "And *that* means you are now in charge of cloud-painting!"

"Okay," Molly laughed, swirling her brush around in a can of paint. *I should have done this a long time ago*, Molly thought as she worked. *I should have gotten involved in school activities and not been so worried about being laughed at.*

It was almost five o'clock when everyone started putting away the supplies and cleaning up the gym. Molly helped put the paint away, then stood in front of the piece of scenery, admiring what she and Sandy had accomplished. Sandy had almost finished the snow-covered fence, and Molly had to admit that her own clouds looked pretty terrific. But the nicest part about the whole afternoon was that she had made some new friends.

Now, if I was just going to the dance, everything would be perfect, Molly thought with a wistful sigh. The Winterland Dance was one of the biggest dances of the whole school year.

But it was silly even to fantasize that Frank would invite her to go with him. After all, they were just science partners, even though Frank had kissed her last night.

Molly reached up and touched her lips, remembering that kiss. If he only thought of her as his science partner, then why had he kissed her? Was it just because, as he had admitted, he liked girls and he liked to flirt?

"Molly, are you ready to go?" Amy asked from behind her.

Molly nodded. They put on their coats and left the gym. As they walked down the corridor that led to the main entrance, Amy exclaimed, "Oh rats! I forgot my math book. I've got to go back to my locker."

"I'll wait for you by the front door," Molly said. She continued on down the hall. As she turned a corner, she saw Frank and a couple of his friends standing outside the boys' gym. They were looking at a poster advertising the upcoming dance. Frank's face immediately lit up when he saw Molly coming toward him.

"What are you doing here so late?" he asked.

"I was working on the decorations for the dance," she told him.

"Let me guess . . . you painted," he said.

She looked at him in surprise. "How did you know?"

He laughed and touched her cheek. "Because you have a smear of blue paint right here."

Molly blushed at his touch. "I was the official cloud-painter," she explained. "Guess I got carried away."

"Hmm, sounds like a very important job," he teased. Then he snapped his fingers. "Oh, wait here. I've got something of yours."

Before Molly could ask him what it was, he disappeared into the gym. As she waited for Frank to return, she smiled shyly at the other two boys. One of them was Jerry Minter, Sandy's boyfriend. The other boy was Ron Williams, a guy Molly didn't know very well.

Just then Amanda Jenkins and her friend Kim Preston came down the hall. "How do you like the poster?" Amanda asked Jerry and Ron. "Kim and I just finished putting them up all over school."

"Looks great," Jerry said.

"Yeah, terrific," Ron added.

Amanda, Kim, Ron, and Jerry chatted for a few minutes while Molly stood silently by. At last Amanda seemed to realize she was there and asked, "How's your science project coming, Molly?"

"Fine," Molly said.

"It's really lucky for Frank that he got you as a partner," Amanda went on with a sly smile. "This time he just might get a passing grade."

At that moment Frank came out of the gym. "This must have dropped out of your backpack yesterday afternoon in my car," he said to Molly, holding out a book.

To her horror Molly saw that it was her paperback romance. For one desperate moment she considered telling him that it wasn't hers, but she knew she couldn't do that. Frank knew it was, and she would look like an idiot if she insisted it wasn't. She felt her cheeks burning as she reached for the book. But before she could take it, Ron grabbed it from Frank.

"What's this?" he asked, then read the title aloud. "*Love's Wild Ways.* Hey, it's a book about love!"

"What are you doing, Molly? Researching romance?" Amanda giggled. Turning to Kim, she said, "Most of us *live* it, but Molly's got to read about it so when it comes along, she'll know exactly how to handle it!"

Kim giggled, too.

"May I have my book, please?" Molly asked stiffly. But instead of giving it to her, Ron opened the novel and flipped through a few pages. " 'Oh, Clarissa,' " he sighed, falling on one knee next to Molly. " 'Clarissa, you're the woman of my dreams. Our passion will overcome all obstacles fate has set in our path!' "

Molly snatched the book out of his hands and ran. Loud laughter followed her down the hall and out the door.

Let me die, she begged silently as she ran, unmindful of the cold air that whipped at her hair and stung her face. They had laughed at her! And the thing that hurt the most was that Frank had laughed at her, too.

What a dope she'd been to think he was anything but a stupid jock! She had actually begun to think he was sensitive and kind, but he wasn't. He was nothing but a creep, and Molly wouldn't have gone to the dance with him even if he'd begged her!

Molly ran all the way home, choking back the tears that threatened to flow.

"Honey, dinner's almost ready," her mother called as Molly entered the front door.

"I'm really not hungry," Molly mumbled as she went into the kitchen. "I think I'll just go out back and do a little work," she said. All she wanted was to escape to the privacy of her shed.

"Molly? Is everything all right?" Mrs. Baker asked.

"Sure. I've just got some things to do. I'll eat later, okay?" Molly forced a smile.

"All right," her mother said. "I'll fix a plate for you. When you get hungry, you can just pop it into the microwave."

Molly nodded and hurried outside to the shed, Sugar romping at her heels.

Once inside, Molly turned on the heater, then collapsed into a chair, tears flooding her eyes. It had finally happened, the thing she'd always feared. The kids had laughed at her. How could they? "How could *he*?" she wailed, thinking of Frank laughing along with the rest of them. A sob caught in her throat, and Sugar whimpered and tried to jump up into her lap, as if trying to comfort her.

Molly picked up the little dog, cuddling him in her arms as tears poured down her face. "Oh, Sugar," she cried, "how could he laugh at me? I thought he really cared about me!" Sugar whimpered again and licked her salty cheek, then jumped down to the floor.

Molly reached for her backpack and pulled out the novel. She stared at the brightly colored cover, the kids' laughter still ringing in her ears. She seized the paperback book in both hands, intent on ripping it to shreds page by page, but then she paused. Why tear it up? Amanda was right. The way things were going, her novels were as close as she'd ever get to real romance.

Chapter Eight

"Molly, what's wrong?" Frank asked the next morning as they constructed a psychrometer. "You've been awfully quiet."

"Nothing's wrong," Molly snapped. "Can you stretch that rubber band tighter?"

He did, a frown on his face. "So how come you're so quiet?"

"I have a lot of things on my mind," Molly replied. She wasn't about to tell him what was really wrong.

"What kind of things?" he persisted.

Molly kept her gaze focused on the work at hand, refusing to look at Frank. He was standing so close, and his after-shave smelled so good. Molly didn't dare look at him because she couldn't bear to see his beautiful brown eyes, or his special smile. It just hurt too much.

"None-of-your-business kinds of things," she retorted.

"Wow, are you ever in one of your prickly moods today!" Frank leaned against the bookshelf and studied her thoughtfully. "Are you mad at me for some reason?" he asked.

"Mad? Me? Whatever gave you that idea?" she muttered sarcastically.

"If you're not mad, how come you won't talk to me, or even look at me?" Frank asked. When she didn't reply, he shrugged. "Well, I guess I'll be going then."

"Go ahead. We're pretty much done here anyway," Molly said, still not looking at him.

"Got anything planned for today?" he asked, not moving.

Molly shrugged. "I guess I'll do what I usually do on Saturdays, which is just hang out."

Frank headed for the door. "Well, I guess I'd better get going. See you tomorrow morning."

Molly nodded, not looking up until she heard the door close behind him.

Molly managed to appear coolly impersonal on Sunday and Monday mornings. Frank seemed surprised on Monday when she told him she would be riding to school with Amy, but when she offered no explanation, he left by himself.

A few minutes later Molly grabbed her backpack and coat as she heard Amy's car horn honk in her driveway.

"So what's up?" Amy asked as soon as Molly got into the car.

"What do you mean?" Molly asked, fastening her seat belt.

"First you run out on me last Friday after school, then Mom gives me the message that you want a ride to school today when every morning for the last week you've been riding with Frank. So, I repeat, what's up?" Amy backed carefully out of Molly's driveway and onto the street.

"I'm sorry about Friday," Molly said. "While I was waiting for you to meet me at the front door, I suddenly remembered I'd promised Mom I'd cook dinner that night so I decided I'd better hurry on home." She didn't like to lie, but she didn't want to tell Amy what had really happened. It was just too embarrassing.

"Why didn't you ride to school with Frank this morning?" Amy asked.

Molly shrugged. "I just didn't feel like it."

Amy shot her a look of disbelief. "The biggest hunk in the whole school, and you don't feel like riding with him? Give me a break!"

"Frank isn't that much of a hunk," Molly said. "I mean, he *is* great-looking, but looks aren't everything. He's just an insensitive clod."

"Hmm, so you guys had a fight," Amy said.

"No, we *didn't* have a fight," Molly protested. "What would we have to fight about? He's only my science partner, not my boyfriend or anything."

Amy glanced over at Molly. "He invited you to go to the Dairy Barn last Thursday night. That doesn't sound like science partners to me. It sounds like a date. You like him, don't you, Molly?"

Molly stared out the car window for a long moment, then nodded miserably. "Yeah, I do," she admitted.

"Then what's the problem?" Amy asked. "I

mean, Frank acts like he likes you, and you say you like him. So what are you doing in my car instead of his?"

Molly sighed. "Because the whole thing is hopeless! Frank and I have nothing in common, and it's crazy for me to think he could ever really care about me. He's my science partner, and that's all he'll ever be."

Amy pulled into an empty space in the school parking lot.

"Come on—let's go before we both get late slips," Molly said, getting out of the car.

"Okay, but I think you're crazy," Amy grumbled, hurrying after Molly as she walked briskly toward the school's main entrance.

Molly tried to ignore Frank during science class, but she could feel his gaze on her during the entire hour. After class she tried to leave before he could catch up with her, but she was unsuccessful.

"Molly," he said, grabbing her shoulder. "Wait a minute."

"What is it, Frank? I don't want to be late for my next class," Molly said, trying not to notice how her heart jumped at the touch of his hand.

"I was just wondering if maybe you'd want to go to the Dairy Barn with me tonight after I get off from work," he said.

Another date . . . he was asking her for another date. As much as the thought thrilled her, Molly knew she couldn't go out with a guy who laughed at her. "I don't think so, Frank," Molly replied. "Thanks anyway."

"But, Molly . . ."

"Look, Frank, I've really got to run." With that, Molly made her escape down the hallway.

Molly was grateful when she didn't see Frank again for the rest of the day, though she couldn't help thinking that maybe Amy was right and she *was* crazy. A gorgeous guy had asked her out, and she had turned him down. She must be out of her mind!

As usual, Amy stayed after school that afternoon to help with the decorations, but Molly didn't. Amanda had probably told everybody that weird Molly the science nerd could only find romance between the covers of a book. They had probably all had a good laugh about it.

Molly walked home alone. The sun was shining, and the snow that had covered the ground was completely gone. *Soon spring will be here,* she thought. Spring meant baseball season, and baseball season reminded her of Frank. But she didn't *want* to be reminded of Frank!

She slowed down as a car pulled up along the curb next to her. She turned and saw Frank. "Get in," he said, leaning over and opening the passenger door.

Molly shook her head.

"Molly, please," he said softly. With a sigh Molly slid into his car. "We need to talk," Frank said as he pulled away from the curb.

"About what?" she asked, although she had a very good idea what he wanted to talk about.

"What's going on? Why are you acting so strange? You've been acting strange for the past three days," Frank told her.

"Maybe I'm acting strange because I *am* strange," Molly replied sharply. "Haven't you heard . . . weird Molly spends all her free time in her little shed studying the weather!"

"Cut it out!" Frank exclaimed, a hint of anger in his voice. He drove for a moment without saying anything, then shot her a curious look. "Does this have something to do with Friday afternoon, when I gave you back your book?"

Molly blushed hotly, too upset to answer.

Frank brought the car to a stop, then turned to face her. "Molly, I'm sorry you got mad," he said earnestly. "We were just fooling around. We didn't mean anything by it."

"But you all laughed at me!" Molly cried, the tremor in her voice signaling the hurt she felt.

"We weren't laughing at *you*," Frank protested. "We were laughing at *Ron* because he was acting like such a dork!"

Molly covered her flaming cheeks with her hands, gazing out the car window because she didn't want to look at Frank. "I was just so embarrassed about the whole thing," she admitted softly.

"Why? Because you read romance novels? Half the girls I know read those things! My mom even reads them!" Frank took one of her hands in his. "Molly, I saw that novel the very first day I came to your shed. Remember? You shoved it into your backpack with a bunch of other papers, but I'd already seen it."

Molly stared at him. "You did?"

"Yeah," he said with that adorable grin. "It's what made me realize there was a lot more to Molly Baker than a sharp mind."

"Oh," Molly whispered. She didn't know what else to say.

"I've been wanting to ask you something, and I guess now is as good a time as any." He looked at her seriously. "Molly, would you go to the Winterland Dance with me?"

All Molly's misery and embarrassment vanished just like last week's snow. As far as she was concerned, it was already spring. "Oh yes, Frank," she cried. "Yes, yes, *yes!*" For the first time Molly was beginning to believe that real life was definitely more wonderful than the kind she read about in her books.

Chapter Nine

"I can't believe the dance is tomorrow night," Sandy Lathrop said to Molly as they worked on the last-minute decorations.

"I'm so excited I know I'll never sleep tonight," Molly admitted, climbing down from the ladder where she had been standing to hang the last of the snowflakes. When she reached the floor, she looked around, awed by how beautiful the gym looked.

It had been transformed into a winter wonderland. Besides the snowflakes hanging from the ceiling and the snow scenes along the walls, there were small trees coated with silver sparkles, and benches surrounded the little skating rink.

Molly closed her eyes, imagining herself in her beautiful new peach-colored velvet dress, gliding across the dance floor in Frank's arms. *Tomorrow night!* she thought with excitement. Tomorrow night all her dreams would come true.

The days since Frank had invited her to the dance had passed quickly. They had finished making all their weather instruments and were now meeting in the mornings only long enough to check the readings, make their predictions, and enter them in their log. They drove to school together every morning, and he called her every evening when he got home from work. At last Molly knew what it was like to have a real boyfriend, and it was more wonderful and more exciting than she'd ever dreamed it could be. *Clarissa and Blake have nothing on Molly and Frank,* she thought dreamily.

"Hey, Molly, you've got that look on your face that tells me you're drifting into the ozone," Sandy said, grinning.

"I was just thinking . . . ," Molly said,

her gaze once again sweeping over the gym.

"It's going to be fun, isn't it?" Sandy exclaimed.

"It's going to be the best night of my life," Molly replied happily. She was so glad she had decided to start working on the decorations committee again. After the incident with the book, she had sworn she'd never go back. But once Frank had convinced her that the kids hadn't been laughing at her after all, she'd been delighted to return.

"I'm home," Molly called as she walked through her front door a while later.

"I'm in the kitchen," her mother called back. "Well, Ms. Sociable, how did the decorating go today?" she asked as Molly came into the kitchen.

"Fantastic," Molly answered, setting her backpack on the floor. "Is there anything I can do to help?"

Mrs. Baker nodded. "You can make a salad."

Molly got out lettuce, tomatoes, and cucumbers and set to work, humming happily.

"You've enjoyed working on the decorations committee, haven't you?" Mrs. Baker observed as she stirred a bubbling pot of goulash.

Molly smiled. "Yeah, it's been a lot of fun. It's funny—I was always afraid that the kids wouldn't accept me. But instead I've made a lot of new friends."

Her mother glanced at her out of the corner of her eye. "And I bet you've discovered that not all pom-pom girls are airheads, and not all athletes are insensitive clods, right? You know, honey, it seems to me that you were just as guilty of pinning labels on people as the other kids were," Mrs. Baker said.

Molly nodded. It had taken one special guy to make her realize that you couldn't judge a book by its cover—unless, she thought, smiling, it happened to be a romance!

At that moment Molly's father arrived, and soon all three were sitting at the table.

"Are you all geared up for this big dance tomorrow night?" Mr. Baker asked, helping himself to a large serving of goulash.

Molly nodded with a happy smile. "I've got a new dress and shoes and a matching purse. I'm as ready as I'll ever be."

Molly toyed with her food, too excited to eat. Tomorrow night at this time, she would be getting dressed for the Winterland Dance. It almost seemed too good to be true!

Chapter Ten

Molly had never taken so much time getting ready for anything as she did for the dance the next evening. She began with a bubble bath. She lay in the strawberry-scented bubbles for nearly an hour, dreaming about how wonderful the night was going to be. After her bath she painted her fingernails and toenails with peach-colored polish that exactly matched her new dress. Then her mother helped her style her hair, arranging it into a mass of soft ringlets.

Next, Molly took special care with her makeup, particularly her mascara, to make her lashes look longer and thicker behind her glasses. *If only I didn't have to wear these things,* she thought with a sigh. But if she wanted to see anything at all, she knew she couldn't do without them, and Molly definitely wanted to see every single thing.

She was thrilled with the way her peach velvet dress looked when she finally put it on. It had an off-the-shoulder neckline, and a short, full skirt that made her legs look longer and her waist appear tiny. Although Molly knew she would never be as beautiful as Amanda Jenkins, she knew she looked pretty good.

"Now, if only I don't mess myself up before Frank gets here," she muttered to herself, looking at her clock and realizing that there was still twenty minutes before he was due to arrive.

Picking up her book from her nightstand, Molly sat down gingerly on the edge of the bed, careful not to wrinkle her dress. She had just a few pages left of *Love's Wild Ways* and was eager to finish it. She opened the paperback and immediately became engrossed in the story. All too soon she had come to the final page.

Blake reached out and took Clarissa in his manly arms. "Clarissa, I don't care who you are or whether you are rich or poor. I love you, and my life will never be complete without you," he murmured.

Clarissa looked deep into his eyes, searching for the truth, and she found it there. His dark eyes were no longer mysterious, but full of love, and as his lips met hers, she realized that their stormy past no longer mattered. All that mattered was their future. And Clarissa knew that her future was here, in his arms.

Molly closed the book with a deep sigh of mingled satisfaction and regret. She always felt a little sad when she finished a novel, as though she were saying a last good-bye to people who had become her special friends.

But tonight there was less sadness, because Molly had a feeling that the book's happy ending was a good omen for her date with Frank. It was going to be a wonderful night, the first of many, she was sure.

Her mother knocked on her door. "Molly?"

"Come on in," Molly answered, standing up and carefully smoothing her skirt.

Mrs. Baker walked in and stopped, clapping her hands with a cry of delight. "Oh, honey, you look absolutely *beautiful*! Turn around and let me see the back."

Molly dutifully whirled around, letting her mother see her from every angle.

"There's only one thing missing," Mrs. Baker said.

"What?" Molly asked, surprised.

"This." Her mother pulled a gold locket out of the pocket of her skirt.

"Oh, Mom," Molly breathed softly.

"With that off-the-shoulder neckline, you definitely need something, and this should do the trick." She motioned for Molly to turn around, then carefully fastened the delicate golden chain around Molly's neck. "There, now you're perfect," she announced.

Molly touched the locket at her throat. She knew it was one of her mother's most treasured possessions—her father had given it to her on their wedding day. "Thanks for letting me wear it, Mom," she said, giving her mother a big hug.

At the sound of the doorbell, Mrs. Baker said, "That must be Frank."

"Are you sure I look okay?" Molly asked nervously, smoothing her skirt once again.

"Much better than okay," her mother assured her. "Now, I'll just try to keep your father from asking Frank too many embarrassing questions." With a reassuring smile Mrs. Baker left the room.

Overcome by a sudden case of the jitters, Molly rechecked her reflection in the mirror and sprayed a little of her favorite cologne on her neck and shoulders. Then, pushing her glasses up from the end of her nose, she headed for the living room, where Frank would be waiting.

When she saw him, her breath caught in her throat. He was sitting on the sofa next to her mother, and he looked incredibly handsome. He was wearing a dark blue suit, a white dress shirt, and a paisley-patterned tie. Molly had never seen him all dressed up before.

Frank stood up as she came into the room, and his gaze locked on her. "Wow!" he said. "You look great!"

Molly blushed. "Thanks," she murmured. "So do you."

"A handsome couple," Molly's mother said, beaming at them both.

"This is for you." Frank handed Molly a white florist's box. Inside she found a corsage of white carnations and baby's breath. As Molly pinned it on, she felt as if she just might burst with excitement and happiness.

"Are you ready?" Frank asked.

She nodded.

"Molly, don't forget your coat. It's quite cold outside," her father said.

Molly took her coat out of the hall closet and threw it over her shoulders, not wanting to crush her pretty corsage.

"Have a wonderful time," her mother said as she walked with them to the front door.

"Thanks, Mrs. Baker, I'm sure we will," Frank replied, opening the door for Molly. As soon as they were in the car, he turned to Molly. "Give me your glasses," he said solemnly.

"What?" Molly stared at him as if he'd lost his mind.

"Give me your glasses," he repeated.

Looking at him curiously, she took off the glasses and handed them to him, then laughed as he pulled a tiny screwdriver out of his breast pocket. "You may be pretty smart,

Molly Baker, but you definitely need somebody to take care of you," he teased as he carefully tightened the screws on each side of her glasses. "Now, try them." He handed them back to her.

Molly put them on and bent her head, delighted when the glasses stayed where they belonged instead of sliding down to the end of her nose. "That's much better," she agreed. "Thanks."

"I can't have my girl's glasses sliding off in the middle of a dance," Frank said, starting the car. His words thrilled Molly. "I hope you like to dance," Frank added as he drove in the direction of the school. "I'm a dancing fool." When Molly didn't respond, he glanced over at her. "Don't tell me you *hate* to dance," he said, seeing her worried expression.

"No, it's not that," she assured him. "It's just that I don't know how to dance very well." That wasn't exactly true. Molly didn't know how to dance *at all*. She'd never been to a dance with a guy before.

Frank laughed. "Oh, that's no problem. I'm an expert teacher. And I'll just bet you're going to be an excellent student, just like you are in school."

"We'll see," Molly replied with a dubious grin.

As Frank pulled into the school parking lot, Molly's sense of anticipation grew. She felt like Cinderella going to the ball, or a character out of one of her novels.

"Wow, everything looks terrific," Frank observed a few minutes later when they entered the gym.

Molly nodded. Although she thought it had looked great the day before, tonight with the band on the stage, the lighting dimmed, and well-dressed couples everywhere, the gym really did look like another world. Frank stopped in front of the piece of scenery that Molly had helped to paint. "This is really nice," he said, then grinned. "Although the clouds look kind of funny."

Molly elbowed him in the side with a look of mock outrage. "They do not!" she protested, though she knew he was just teasing her.

At that moment Sandy and Jerry came over to them. Sandy looked very glamorous in a purple sequined dress with a tulle skirt. "Admiring our handiwork?" she asked Frank, gesturing at the scenery. "Molly and I are thinking about moving to New York City and becoming artists, right, Molly?" Molly laughed.

"You'd starve," Jerry announced, causing Sandy to make a face at him. "Have you guys seen the skating rink yet?"

Frank shook his head. "We just walked in."

"I'm trying to get Sandy to skate with me, but she won't," Jerry said.

"Like I'm really going to try to skate in this outfit," Sandy scoffed. "Besides, the rink isn't meant for skating. It's just supposed to look like a frozen pond."

At that moment the band began to play. Frank grabbed Molly's hand. "They're playing our song," he said, pulling her onto the dance floor where several couples had begun dancing. "Just sort of move around to the beat of the music," he instructed. "The good thing about fast dancing is that there is no right or wrong way to do it. As long as you keep moving, it's okay."

Molly did as she was told, watching the other people on the floor and copying their steps. *This is easy,* she marveled, smiling at Frank.

The next song was a slow one. Frank

pulled Molly into his arms, and her heart beat so loudly she was sure he would be able to hear it. "Your dress feels nice," he said as he rubbed his hand over the velvet at her waist. His arms felt so strong around her, and Molly could feel his warm breath on her cheek. She would have been happy to remain in his arms on the dance floor forever. There was no doubt about it—Molly was hopelessly in love with Frank Sanders.

As the evening progressed, they danced almost every dance, and each time Molly grew more confident, more at ease. Between dances they talked with their friends and sampled the refreshments. Amy was there with Craig, and the four of them spent a lot of time together. Frank either held Molly's hand or kept his arm around her waist. It was as if he wanted everyone to know that she was his girl. Even when Amanda slunk up to them in her form-fitting black dress, Frank was pleasant to her, but not at all flirtatious, and he kept a firm grip on Molly's hand. She had never been happier in her life.

The dance was nearly over when Molly made her way through the crowd to the rest room to check her makeup. Surprised to find herself alone, she took her lipstick out of her purse and applied a fresh coat, smiling dreamily at her reflection. Then Molly decided to go into the privacy of a stall to adjust her slip. She'd just latched the door when she heard some other girls walk in.

"Oh rats, I forgot my lipstick. Can I borrow yours?"

Molly immediately recognized Amanda Jenkin's voice.

"Sure, here you go," a second feminine voice replied, one Molly didn't recognize.

As Molly fixed her slip, she paid no attention to the girls' conversation—until she suddenly heard her name.

"I didn't know Frank Sanders was dating Molly Baker," the unidentified voice said.

"Oh, he's not really," Amanda replied airily. "He's just seeing her until after the science fair."

"What do you mean? Why would he do that?" the other girl asked.

"Frank was flunking science, and the coach told him that if he didn't get his grade up, he would be kicked off the team. So Frank talked Mr. Welsh into giving him Molly as his partner. You know, she *is* the best student in the class." Molly stood as though she had been frozen to the spot. "He's just dating her to keep her happy until after the science fair," Amanda went on. "All Frank wants from Molly Baker is a good grade so he can play baseball."

"That's sort of mean, isn't it?" the other girl said.

"Who cares? The team needs Frank if we're going to make it into the play-offs this year. He's the best hitter we have," Amanda replied.

Molly heard the sound of a purse snapping shut. "Come on, we'd better get back there," the other girl said. The door opened and closed once again, and the rest room was silent.

Molly still couldn't move. Her dream date had suddenly turned into a nightmare.

Chapter Eleven

Molly was completely stunned by what she'd just heard. There was no doubt in her mind that it was true. Everything Amanda had said made only too much sense. Of course Frank was just using her. Why else would he date someone like her? How had she managed to convince herself that he really cared about her? The whole thing was so awful that it made Molly sick to her stomach.

She came out of the stall and stared at her reflection. "For someone who's supposed to be smart, you sure are a dummy," she said to the girl in the mirror, her voice trembling.

Oh yes, she was dumb, all right. She'd actually believed that she and Frank were developing a strong, wonderful relationship. How could she have been so stupid?

Molly wished with all her heart that she never had to see Frank Sanders again. She wanted to hide in the rest room forever, but of course she had to go back out there and pretend that everything was okay.

Taking a deep breath, Molly closed her eyes and clenched her fists. Then she walked back to the gym.

Immediately Frank came up to her. "I wondered where you'd disappeared to," he said, smiling. "They're getting ready to play the last dance." He took her by the elbow and led her onto the floor.

Molly didn't want to dance with him and feel his arms wrapped warmly around her, but she also didn't want to make a scene.

The music was slow and romantic. Molly knew she'd never hear that song again without thinking of this night and her last dance with Frank. He held her close, and Molly closed her eyes, memorizing everything about him. She wanted to remember every single thing about this moment, because after tonight, nothing would ever be the same between them.

She knew she should hate him, but right now all she felt was an overwhelming sadness, a hurt too deep for anger.

"Are you having a good time?" Frank asked, gazing down at her.

"Sure," she answered. How could he look at her that way, as if he really cared about her? *He should be an actor instead of a baseball player,* she thought.

"Some of the kids are going out to eat after the dance. You want to join them?" he asked.

"Not really," Molly replied. She knew she couldn't keep this up much longer. "In fact, I'm not feeling very well. I'd just like to go home."

"You're not feeling well? What's wrong?" Frank looked at her with what appeared to be real concern.

I have a heartache, she thought, but that wasn't what she said. "My stomach is kind of upset," she told him truthfully. "I really want to go home."

"Okay," Frank said as the song came to an end. He sounded disappointed.

It took them nearly fifteen minutes to collect Molly's coat and make their way out of the gym. They said good-bye to all their friends, then got into Frank's car. While they waited for the heater to warm up, Molly pulled her coat more tightly around her neck, not caring anymore if she crushed her corsage.

"I hope you're not getting the flu or anything," Frank said as he pulled out of the parking lot. "I wouldn't want you to be sick next week for the science fair."

"Oh, don't worry about that. I'm sure I'll be just fine," Molly assured him. For the first time since overhearing the conversation in the rest room, she was feeling the stirrings of anger.

"I think we're going to do really well, don't you?" Frank asked, reaching out to take her hand. "We make a pretty good team." He smiled at her and again Molly thought it was a shame he wasn't an actor. His performance over these past three weeks would earn him an Academy Award!

She sighed with relief as he pulled into her driveway. *Thank goodness this nightmare is almost over,* she thought. Frank unbuckled his seat belt and turned to face her. "If you're feeling better tomorrow, you want to do something? Maybe we could go to a movie."

"I don't think so," Molly replied. "I've got a really busy weekend planned. I think we may be going to my aunt's house."

"But what about our weather predictions?"

"I'll make them," she said, then added quickly, "In fact, I can do it for the rest of the week. There's no reason for you to keep coming over to my house every morning. Then on Thursday my dad will drive all our stuff to school for the fair on Friday."

"That doesn't seem right," Frank said with a frown. "This was supposed to be a fifty-fifty deal."

"It's just a couple more days. We've worked together on everything. I really don't mind." In fact, this was the way she wanted it. She never wanted to see him alone again.

"Well, I'll still come by to drive you to school," he said.

Molly shook her head. "I'm riding with Amy next week—we've already made plans. But thanks anyway."

"Then I'll call you Sunday night, after you get back from your aunt's," he said firmly. "I can't go two or three days without talking to my girl." He smiled and started to lean forward. Molly knew he was going to kiss her, and if he did, she knew she would burst into tears. She quickly unfastened her seat belt, opened her door, and jumped out of the car.

"Thanks, Frank. I had a wonderful time." Before he had a chance to say or do anything, Molly ran to the house. She slipped inside and waited at the door until she heard his car drive off down the street.

Molly was grateful that her parents were in bed. The house was dark and quiet as she tiptoed to her room. She quickly pulled off her clothes, changed into her nightgown, and crawled into bed, not bothering to wash her face.

She lay on her back and stared up at her darkened ceiling, too hurt and angry even to cry.

Why hadn't she realized the game Frank had been playing? Why hadn't she seen how he was using her?

Now the tears finally began to fall, trickling down her face and into her ears. Terrific! Not only had Frank Sanders broken her heart, she'd probably get an ear infection from lying on her back and crying over him!

Molly turned over on her side, remembering how excited she'd been before the dance had begun. What a fool she'd been to imagine that the happy ending to Clarissa and Blake's story meant a happy ending for her as well. Happily-ever-after only happened in romance novels. In real life, romance was nothing but a big pain in the heart!

Chapter Twelve

It was the longest, most difficult weekend Molly had ever endured. Her mother knew something was wrong, but when Molly said she'd rather not discuss it, Mrs. Baker respected her privacy and didn't insist. Molly was glad. It was much too painful to discuss with anyone, even her mom.

But by Monday morning, in addition to her broken heart, Molly was nursing a healthy case of rage. How *dare* Frank use her, pretend to like her just to stay on the baseball team! Who did Frank Sanders think he was? If she didn't want that internship so badly, she'd be tempted to mess up the science project on purpose. That would fix him! It would be exactly what he deserved. But Molly knew that any such action would only hurt herself as well, and not even sweet revenge was worth losing a chance at the internship.

She wasn't exactly sure how she should react when she saw Frank again. He'd called Sunday night as he'd said he would, but she hadn't spoken to him. She'd asked her mother to tell him she couldn't come to the phone.

Molly finally decided the best thing to do was simply to act as if she didn't like him anymore. At least that way she could retain some of her bruised pride.

"How come you're not riding to school with Frank this morning?" Amy asked as she drove Molly to school. "I thought you two had become a really hot item."

"I've decided I really don't like him much after all," Molly replied.

"How come?" Amy asked incredulously.

"He's just not my type," Molly said. "Did you have a good time at the dance with Craig?"

"Wonderful!" Amy said. To Molly's relief, she

spent the rest of the drive to school talking about Craig's many charms.

Molly was surprised and relieved when she got to science class and discovered that Frank wasn't there. She was glad because she wasn't ready to face him yet, though she hoped he wasn't sick.

He wasn't in class on Tuesday, either. But on Wednesday he showed up again. When class was over, Molly ran for the exit to avoid talking to him. But she didn't run fast enough, because he caught up and fell into step next to her. "Have you missed me?" he asked with that smile that still made Molly's heart beat faster.

"Not really," Molly returned coolly. Now was as good a time as any to let Frank know she didn't want anything more to do with him.

Frank apparently thought she was teasing, because he laughed. "I'm sorry I haven't called or anything. I've been spending most of my time these last couple of days with my folks—we had to move Grandma to a new nursing home where she could get more individual care, and she's having a hard time adjusting to the change," he said. They stopped at the door of Molly's English classroom. "You want to go to the Dairy Barn with me tonight?"

"I don't want to go anywhere with you ever again!" Molly replied, her anger suddenly boiling to the surface.

Frank stared at her in shock. "Excuse me?"

"I don't like being used," Molly retorted.

"Molly, I don't know what you're talking about," Frank said, his forehead wrinkled.

Molly glared at him furiously. "Just answer one question. Were you going to be dropped from the baseball team because of your science grade?" she asked.

"Yeah, but . . ."

"And did you ask Mr. Welsh to assign me as your partner for the fair?" she interrupted.

"Well, sort of, but . . ."

Molly didn't let him say another word. He'd already said more than enough to confirm that Amanda had been telling the truth. "Look, Frank, I know you used me to make sure you got a good grade in science. You don't have to be nice to me anymore. I don't ever want to see or talk to you again!" Molly whirled around and stomped into her classroom. Frank started to follow her, but stopped as the bell rang. Molly breathed a sigh of relief when he hurried off to his own class. *Well, that's that,* she thought. She'd told Frank Sanders off. He knew he couldn't play her for a fool any longer. She'd settled the whole thing. But why did she still feel so bad?

"Oh, honey, look! You won!" Molly's mother hugged her as all three Bakers stood in front of Molly and Frank's exhibit at the science fair. A blue ribbon was fastened to one of the weather charts.

"It looks like our little girl is going to that fancy weather school this summer," Mr. Baker said, grinning.

Molly nodded. She knew she should feel ecstatic, and she was proud, but her heart was as heavy as lead. She was getting what she wanted, and Frank had gotten what he wanted. So why couldn't she get him out of her mind? Why was every minute of every day so miserable?

Since Wednesday, Frank had kept his distance. But she'd felt his eyes on her during science class and whenever they passed each other in the halls. What confused Molly more than anything was that although she knew she should hate Frank, she just couldn't. In spite of everything, she still cared about him.

Later that afternoon, after she and her parents had returned from the science fair, Molly went out to her shed. It seemed strangely empty without the clutter of the homemade weather instruments.

She sat down and absently scratched Sugar behind his ears, listening to the rain falling on the roof. It had started to rain just minutes after they had gotten home from the fair, and according to Molly's calculations, it wasn't going to end until tomorrow.

It somehow seemed appropriate for it to be raining. The dreary weather matched Molly's mood. "So what do you want to do today, Sugar?" she said. Then suddenly Sugar jumped up and danced over to the door, barking with excitement.

Molly got up and followed him. Opening the door, she was astonished to see Frank standing there. "I want to talk to you," he said grimly.

"Go away," she snapped. "I don't want to talk to *you*!" She started to shut the door, but Sugar ran outside and jumped all over

Frank. "Sugar, get in here," Molly yelled, but the little dog ignored her. "Okay, fine. Stay out there in the rain. See if I care," she muttered, slamming the door and leaving both Sugar and Frank outside.

"Molly, I'm going to stay out here until you let me talk to you," Frank shouted through the closed door.

"Then you're going to be out there a very long time," Molly shouted back. She sat back down in her chair. They had nothing at all to talk about. Why couldn't he just leave her alone?

Molly got up again and looked outside. Frank was still standing in the rain, Sugar frisking around his feet. *Traitor,* she thought, glaring at the little dog. He was getting soaked. So was Frank, but she didn't care. She didn't care if he got the worst cold of his life and sneezed himself silly!

She went back over to her chair and sat down again. The rain, which had been pattering softly on the roof, began to beat harder. Again Molly went over to the window. Frank's hair was plastered to his head and his jacket was drenched.

Flinging the door open, she yelled, "You're crazy!"

"I told you I wasn't leaving until we talk," he said. "I'll stay here all night if that's what it takes. I'll stand here through a blizzard or a tornado!"

Molly gave up. "You'd better come in before you catch pneumonia."

He ran for the shed, Sugar right behind him. Once they were inside, they both shook themselves, pelting Molly with raindrops. Sugar ran to his bed in the corner and Frank took off his wet coat, then faced Molly. "We need to get something straightened out," he said.

"I think things *are* straightened out," she answered sharply. Even though she wanted to hate him, being so close to him made her heart pound wildly.

"No, everything's totally messed up, and I'm not sure why." Frank moved even closer to her, so close that she could see the golden flecks in his brown eyes. "Molly, I thought we really had something special between us."

"Oh, Frank, stop it," Molly said wearily. "At the dance I overheard a conversation. Somebody said that the only reason you were dating me was to keep me happy so I'd do a good job on the science project and you'd get a good grade so you could stay on the baseball team. You don't have to pretend anymore. The fair is over. You're on the team."

Frank shook his head. "I don't know who said that, but whoever it was, they didn't know what they were talking about." He put his hands on her shoulders. "I'll admit, you were right about a few things. I would have been dropped from the team if I didn't bring up my science grade, and I *did* ask Mr. Welsh if you could be my partner."

Molly tried to pull away, but he held her tightly. "Molly, you told me at the very beginning that you intended to win first prize with or without my help. So why would I date you just to make sure you did a good job? You always do a good job." His eyes were so soft, so warm, as they gazed into hers. "From the moment I saw that romance book, I knew you weren't only interested in the weather! And the more time we spent together, the more I realized what a terrific person you are. I wasn't *pretending* to like you, Molly. I *do* like you—a lot. I don't care about the science fair, or my grade. All I really care about is you." And to Molly's delighted astonishment, he bent his head and pressed his lips to hers in a long, sweet kiss. "Can we start all over again?" he asked when they finally came up for air.

All Molly could do was nod. She was so happy that she thought she might explode.

"And there's one more thing," Frank went on. "I've decided I'd really like to take advantage of that second internship we won. Only this time, I don't want you to be just my science partner. I want you to be my girl."

"I think that could be arranged," Molly whispered. As Frank kissed her again, she started to giggle.

He looked down at her, puzzled. "What's so funny?"

"My glasses—they're getting all steamed up!" she said.

"Then let's take them off." Very gently Frank removed her glasses and set them on the workbench. "I love you, Green Eyes," he said softly.

And as he kissed her a third time, Molly realized that predicting the weather wasn't nearly as difficult as predicting love.

Sweet Dreams

SWEET DREAMS are fresh, fun and exciting--alive with the flavor of the contemporary teen scene--the joy and doubt of first love. If you've missed any SWEET DREAMS titles, then you're missing out on your kind of stories, written about people like you!

ALL-STAR MOVIE
AND TV FAVORITES

The Hottest Teen Heartthrobs!

These terrific star bios are packed with the juicy details *you* want to know. Here's the inside scoop on the star's family life, friends, tips on dating, life on the set, future career plans, *plus* fantastic photo inserts.